# AN INQUIRY INTO THE
# ASSASSINATION OF ABRAHAM LINCOLN

*Works by Emmett McLoughlin*

Books: People's Padre
American Culture and Catholic Schools
Crime and Immorality in the Catholic Church

Film: Portrait of an Ex-Priest

Recordings: Priest to Citizen
As The Twig Is Bent
No Short Cut to Heaven
Freemasonry—America's Sleeping Giant

# *An inquiry into the assassination of* ABRAHAM LINCOLN

by
EMMETT McLOUGHLIN

THE CITADEL PRESS    SECAUCUS, N.J.

First paperbound printing, 1977
Copyright © 1963 by Emmett McLoughlin
All rights reserved
Published by Citadel Press
A division of Lyle Stuart Inc.
120 Enterprise Ave., Secaucus, N.J. 07094
In Canada: George J. McLeod Limited, Toronto, Ont.
Manufactured in the United States of America
ISBN 0-8065-0605-9

# DEDICATION

*To Ralph Watkins of Buckeye, Arizona, a most proven friend who, like Abraham Lincoln, has struggled from the poverty of the Midwest to success in business and government, and who, in a lifetime of service to his country, to his friends, and to his neighbors, has never forgotten the "log cabin" of his boyhood.*

"What is likely to bring disfavor, get others to do."
>Rev. Baltasar Gracian,
>Society of Jesus, 1653

"My History of the Jesuits, is in 4 Vol. in twelves, printed at Amsterdam in 1761. The Work is anonymous; because, as I suppose, the Author was afraid as all the Monarks of Europe were at that time, of Jesuitical Assassination."
>John Adams to
>Thomas Jefferson,
>Nov. 4, 1816

"I believe he is protected by the clergy, and that the murder is the result of a deep laid plot, not only against the life of President Lincoln, but against the existence of the republic, as we are aware that priesthood and royalty are and always have been opposed to liberty. That such men as Surratt, Booth, Wiechman, and others, should, of their own accord, plan and execute the infernal plot which resulted in the death of President Lincoln, is impossible."
>Henri Sainte-Marie,
>Affidavit to the American
>Legation in Rome, July 10, 1866

"A conspiracy is rarely, if ever, proved by positive testimony. When a crime of high magnitude is about to be perpetrated by a combination of individuals, they do not act openly, but covertly and secretly. The purpose formed is known only to those who enter into it. Unless one of the original conspirators betray his companions and give evidence against them, their guilt can be proved only by circumstantial evidence.

"It is said by some writers on evidence that such circumstances are stronger than positive proof. A witness swearing positively, it is said, may misapprehend the facts or swear falsely, but that circumstances can not lie."
>Special Judge Advocate
>John A. Bingham, quoted in
>*The Trial of the Conspirators,*
>Washington, 1865

# Table of Contents

| | |
|---|---|
| **Preface** | 7 |
| *Part One: The Background* | |
| 1. The Shot That Echoes Unceasingly | 13 |
| 2. The Theory That Justified the Act | 29 |
| 3. Backdrop for Treason | 38 |
| 4. Conspiracy South of the Border | 64 |
| 5. The Man and the Demi-God | 89 |
| *Part Two: The Crime* | |
| 6. A Man Is Shot | 103 |
| 7. The Hired Hands: A Motley Crew | 107 |
| 8. The Ancient Privilege of Sanctuary | 129 |
| 9. The Trial of John Surratt | 145 |
| 10. Epilogue | 158 |
| Appendix: | |
|    Excerpts from the Words of Two Men | 165 |
|    Notes | 173 |
|    Bibliography | 179 |
| **Index** | 186 |

SURRATT AS A PAPAL ZOUAVE

# Preface

Among the many pleasant compensations for openly going A.W.O.L. from the Pope's army of the priesthood is the volume of informative and provocative friendly mail one receives. It more than atones, at least in spirit, for the thousands of damning, obscene, and threatening letters from the sickeningly devout laity and the smug, self-sanctified clergy.

In 1955 I received a letter "from one heretic to another." It came from one Albert Bailey of Drexel Hill, Pennsylvania. His father had been a contemporary of Abraham Lincoln and had edited a weekly paper. It had covered the Civil War Draft Riots of 1863 which, he said, were properly called the "Irish Draft Riots." This surprised me, as I had always been taught that Catholics, especially the Irish, were the solid-rock foundation of American loyalty.

But the jolt in his letter was the statement that his father had told him that the Roman Catholics were deeply involved in the assassination of Abraham Lincoln. This I had never heard before.

My reaction was a hangover from the spoonfed type of history I had received in Catholic schools. We had had only the sketchiest concept of Lincoln's assassination.

In fact, many Catholic history books of a generation or two ago (and this still holds true today) did not mention his murder at all.

I began to search. A Masonic scholar suggested books confirming the Catholic involvement in the killing, but added as even more surprising: "For some strange reason, the Jesuits were able to suppress publicizing of their part in the conspiracy, and this is the more remarkable because at that time—the Civil War era—the Roman Catholics were not numerically strong, even in New York, Boston, Philadelphia, and Baltimore."

It was about this time that a friend gave me an old book entitled *Fifty Years in the Church of Rome*.[1] Its author was the most famous ex-priest in American history, Charles Chiniquy. When he left the Church, after particularly vicious treatment at the hands of Bishop O'Regan of Chicago, some 25,000 Catholics followed him.

Chiniquy tells how, in 1856, in the state of Illinois, he was dragged into court, at the instigation of the bishop. Accused of the usual morals charge, the ex-priest was defended against the charges being vigorously pressed by representatives of the Church. The defense attorney was a warm and brilliant local lawyer, one Abraham Lincoln. Thus began an enduring friendship during which the ex-priest visited Lincoln in the White House and frequently warned him of the Church's antagonism and of its threats to the very life of the President.

Chiniquy's detailed prophesy of assassination and his indictment of the Catholic Church will naturally be dismissed by Catholic writers as biased, bigoted, and untruthful, because its author was an ex-priest. It is strange

### Preface

how anyone who leaves the Catholic priesthood is by that fact convicted of being a mental and moral degenerate, which makes him incapable of telling the truth, while ex-Communists or ex-Protestants (like Louis Budenz or Dale Francis) who embrace the Catholic Church, no matter how shallow their backgrounds, when they shift to Rome, seem to have drunk at the wellspring of papal infallibility itself. They are to be believed implicitly, because "they have been there."

But I did not rest with Chiniquy. On lecture tours, at medical meetings, at hospital conventions, I asked everyone who would listen what they knew about the role of the Catholic Church in the murder of Lincoln. A few had heard of Chiniquy's book. As I propounded my gradually growing array of facts, most of my listeners were as astounded as I had been.

It was then that I determined to learn whether the Catholic Church had actually been involved in the death of Lincoln. I searched libraries in San Francisco, Los Angeles, Kansas City, Toledo, Columbus, Erie, Cleveland, Boston, New York, and at the University of Arizona. Friends assembled catalogs from rare book stores in America and Europe. I strained my knowledge of Spanish to study in the archives of the Roosevelt Library and the Biblioteca Nacional in Mexico City. After all Abraham Lincoln was a contemporary of Emperor Maximilian, the ruler foisted upon Mexico during our Civil War by Napoleon III, Emperor Franz Joseph of Austria, and Pope Pius IX. Lincoln's administration had been friendly to Juarez and had condemned the enthronement of Maximilian as a flagrant violation of the Monroe Doctrine.

## Preface

I found that the encyclicals of Pius IX referred to by Chiniquy were unavailable in English or even in the Latin of the semi-official *Enchiridion*. I found them in Spanish volumes in the Peruvian Biblioteca Nacional in Lima.

By a strange coincidence, as leads pointed to books critical of the Catholic Church and particularly of the Jesuits, I discovered that they were usually "out of print," no matter how recently they had been published. But Mrs. Helen Miller of Phoenix Public Library, working through the Inter-Library Loan Service, scoured the country and usually found them, frequently in the Library of Congress in Washington, D.C.

Norman Meese, Thirty-third Degree Mason and editor of *New Age*, the official organ of the Supreme Council of the Southern Jurisdiction of the Scottish Rite of Freemasonry, was of very great assistance in suggesting other out-of-print books from Lincoln's time.

The search has lasted many years. The following pages present the facts as I have found them. The bibliography will aid the reader who wishes to check my research; it will furthermore indicate that my work was by no means confined to the study of anti-Catholic literature.

It is an amazing story, and one that I invite the reader to check for himself. I am convinced that any reader who approaches the subject with an interest in the discovery of the truth, let the chips fall where they may, will be compelled to accept the overwhelming evidence that points to the complicity of the Church in the instigation, the plotting, and the murder of the Great Emancipator.

# PART ONE

# The Background

Chapter One

# The Shot That Echoes Unceasingly

As I write, America is fast approaching the first centennial of one of its saddest and most tragic days in history. On April 14, 1865, a shot was fired in Ford's Theater, in the nation's capital, and after a night of anxiety and pain, the President of the United States succumbed, a victim of the bullet of an assassin. The man who had led these United States through the years of greatest peril lay dead at the moment of triumph.

Walt Whitman, beloved poet of American freedom, was to weep in song that schoolchildren would not tire of repeating:

>*The ship has weathered every rack,*
>*The prize we sought is won,*
>*The port is near, the bells I hear,*
>*The people all exulting,*
>*While follow eyes the steady keel,*
>*The vessel grim and daring;*
>*But O heart! heart! heart!*
>*O the bleeding drops of red,*
>*Where on the deck my Captain lies,*
>*Fallen cold and dead.*

PRESIDENT LINCOLN'S FUNERAL—BURIAL SERVICE AT OAK RIDGE, SPRINGFIELD, ILLINOIS
[Sketched by W. Waud.]

## The Shot That Echoes Unceasingly

Thomas Nast, famed artist of *Harper's Weekly*, entitled his steel-engraved drawings of Lincoln's funeral cortege "Our Savior," "Our Martyred President," and "Liberty's Great Martyr."

And Herman Melville, great novelist of the mid-years of the nineteenth century, was not less stricken with grief:

> *There is sobbing of the strong,*
> *And a pall upon the land;*
> *But the People in their weeping*
> *Bare the iron hand;*
> *Beware the People weeping*
> *When they bare the iron hand.*

A century has passed, and the shot on the night of the 14th of April, 1865, continues to reverberate through the halls of time, as surely as the shot at Sarajevo in 1914 is still to be heard around the world.

America, these United States, was temporarily disunited in a great, a tragic, and a bloody struggle, one that would leave in its wake personal and social tragedies for many decades, and that would at the same time capture the imagination of the people, fascinate historians and public alike, and in short have repercussions in the worlds of politics and of scholarship greater than any other event in the first one hundred and fifty years in the life of the nation.

The sobbing has ceased, and all the principal actors, and the minor ones as well, in this national tragedy are now gone from the scene, yet not one of them is allowed to rest peacefully in a grave. Volume after volume comes pouring from the pens of scholars, historians, students of American history—volumes that reveal new facts, suggest new speculations, offer conjecture and compound the riddle and the confusion surrounding the assassination of the great folk-hero of nineteenth century America.

Under the microscope of historians, no aspect of the tragedy remains unstudied, no actor in the drama is free from analytic and often condemnatory review. Did Mary Lincoln live in poverty, a President's widow deeply concerned over money, because she was subject to blackmail, it is asked. Was Jefferson Davis the instigator of the crime? Or Vice-President Johnson? Or Lincoln's cabinet members, his Secretary of State or his Secretary of War? Did John Wilkes Booth really die in the home of the Garretts?

Some contend that the conspirators were sympathizers of the Confederacy, if not actual spies and hired hands of Confederate leaders; whether bitter with the taste of defeat, or mercenary as paid hands of rebel leaders, one can only guess, but in either instance they were motivated by close connection with the secessionists.

Others argue that the assassin and whatever conspirators he might have had were hired by Northern sympathizers who were dissatisfied with the pace of Lincoln's proposed Reconstruction movement, who felt that Lincoln would be compromising in an effort to mend the Union that had been torn asunder.

Thus a voluminous library has been built up over the years; a library on every aspect and detail of the Civil War. It is so large and detailed that one could not hope to read each word if one were to devote years to reading.

### The Shot That Echoes Unceasingly

And in this great scholarship, the assassination of Lincoln continues to hold the reader spellbound, continues to have a central and fascinating interest. It is a tragic climax that has been studied minute by minute, each sideroad and bypath pursued with most exacting detail. No aspect of this event can be said to be enshrouded in silence.

No aspect in silence—save one! Books hundreds of pages in length continue to roll off the presses, books that delve into every phase of the conspiracy that preceded the assassination and the trials that followed it, books that are strangely silent on one and only one phase: *the role of the Catholic Church at that crucial moment in American history.*

It is the thesis of this book that the Roman Catholic Church was deliberately and culpably involved in the assassination of President Lincoln. Involvement can take on many forms, and each will be spelled out in the pages that follow. The Church was involved by its sympathy for the Confederate cause and for slavery, which sympathy gave encouragement, spiritual leadership, and guidance to the assassins. It was involved by its theoretical position on the forcible removal of heads of states whom it considered inimical and heretical, and by its history of aiding and abetting such removals, including by assassination, in Latin America.

The Church was involved in that several of the conspirators were among her adherents, devout and devoted before, during, and after the fatal event. The Church was further involved by the post factum approval of the firing of the bullet that killed Lincoln. Finally, the Catholic Church, in Canada, in England, and in its seat of

## THE BACKGROUND

power, the Vatican, gave aid, refuge, sanctuary, and protection to one of the conspirators, concealed his presence, harbored him from the demanding hand of the American authorities, and assisted his final but unsuccessful effort to escape from trial.

In brief and in summary, it will be shown in these pages that this involvement included the leadership in the Vatican, the sentiments of its clergy and its laity, especially its Irish adherents in America, and the actions of its members.

Historians point out that there are many puzzling, unanswered questions in the story of the Lincoln murder. Why wasn't the President effectively guarded on the night of April 14, 1865? Why was Booth's escape route unpatrolled? Why was the Army so slow in following known leads? Why did Booth want to see Vice-President Johnson on that Good Friday? Why was the Vice-President so drunk the next day?

Why were the captured conspirators kept hooded? Why were they kept in such complete solitary confinement, even from each other?

The questions are endless, and the rumors are as fantastic as can be expected when shrewd, accomplished conspirators hire others to execute their plans. The most recent attempt to throw historical bloodhounds off the track is the widely publicized insinuation, spread during the Civil War Centennial, that Lincoln's Secretary of War Stanton masterminded the assassination because Lincoln was not vindictive enough against the defeated Confederate leaders.

This book does not claim that Roman Catholics or their

## The Shot That Echoes Unceasingly

Hierarchy were the sole villains in the piece. It contends, rather, that the Catholic Church and the Southern Confederates, acting in Richmond, in Maryland, and in Canada, were conspirators in crime, possibly unwittingly; that the Catholic Church was the silent partner; and that the Hierarchy hid on the sidelines, as the Jesuits had done for centuries, guided by the principle: "What is likely to bring disfavor get others to do."

It is the further contention of this book that only after the murder did the Roman Catholic Hierarchy openly show its sympathy in its attempts to save the arrested conspirators and in concealing John Surratt and smuggling him into the Pope's Zouave army.

Finally, it is the contention of this book that the preponderance of circumstantial evidence points more strongly to the guilt of the Roman Catholic Church than it does to any of the other suspects in the plot.

"What could have been the motive of the Church in wanting Lincoln assassinated?" This was the question most frequently asked when people learned that I was chasing down leads all over the world.

There are several motives, strikingly similar and no less strong than those that had prompted the Vatican's hired inquisitors and personal agents to commit murder on countless occasions before. Among these, none is quite so specific in singling out Lincoln as an enemy of the Roman Catholic Church as his association, in the capacity of legal counsel, with the so-called renegade, Charles Chiniquy.

## THE BACKGROUND

Abraham Lincoln's defense in the court in Urbana, Illinois, in 1857, of the rebellious ex-priest, Charles Chiniquy, from the schemes of Bishop O'Regan of Chicago, was reason enough to bring down upon the Great Emancipator the full fury of the Vatican. The brilliant defense by Lincoln served to lift the veil behind which there lurked the greed and immorality of bishops and priests alike. This event is related in detail in the ex-priest's book, and it is confirmed by Sandburg in his monumental study of the life of Lincoln.[1] Yet, important as it was in the development of Lincoln and in an understanding of the events leading up to his death, it is usually not to be found—not even the slightest mention of it—in books dealing with almost every aspect of the life of the President.

Abraham Lincoln's dramatic proclamation, by which he declared Negro slaves in secessionist states to be free, provided still another reason why Catholics, especially the Irish Catholic immigrants in this country, wanted to see the Great Emancipator liquidated. In fact, it was on this very issue of slavery, and the strong position taken against the continuation and extension of the slave system by the North, that many of these Catholics wanted to see the entire Union liquidated. Thus, only ten days after the crucial Battle of Gettysburg, the Catholics in America were making efforts to defeat and dissolve the Union—efforts the details of which are told in the pages of this book.

The Roman Church makes much, in the indoctrination of Catholic students, of the history of Our Lady of Ransom and the monks of the Middle Ages who labored to free the Christians enslaved by the Mohammedans in Northern Africa. But idealistic Catholic youngsters, such as I was, are not taught that the Vatican approved—both by open collusion and by tacit acceptance—the resumption of the slave trade in Africa on the part of the Church-dominated regime in Portugal in 1444, and the Church raised only the mildest whimpers of protest against the profitable continuation of the slave trade for some four hundred years thereafter, justifying its position on the grounds that slavery gave the African natives a boon greater than freedom—an opportunity to become adherents of the One True Faith.

Never have I seen a history book used in the parochial schools that stated that the Indians in Mexico were made chattels, "encomendados" placed in bondage and held in thralldom after Cortez conquered Montezuma. At that time, all of the natives were enslaved, except for the caciques or the chieftans, and they were murdered unless they helped in turn to enslave their own people. The Church not only approved, it participated in the enslavement process; its participation was not tacit or silent, it was vocal and explicit.

Slavery was the fate of the once-magnificent Inca civilization of Peru, Bolivia, and Ecuador, when the explorers and exploiters came with their guns and their Bibles, their military personnel and their priests. And today, several centuries later, in a more subtle form slavery continues to be practiced, modified only in that the chattels have been changed to a system of abject poverty amid the splendor and wealth of the Church.

So that, far from having become friendly to Lincoln

as a result of his emancipating acts, the Church, rooted as it was in a tradition sympathetic to slavery, was only further alienated from the President.

But the most compelling motive for the elimination of Abraham Lincoln was that he was the world's most powerful personification of that heresy—that apostasy which was the most serious threat in history to the Roman Catholic Church, its existence and its power—Protestantism.

The papacy was still reeling from the violent and bloody defeats it had suffered at the hands of the French Revolutionists in 1789. Its book burners and the compilers of its Index of Forbidden Books were hard put to chase down the iconoclastic writings of the Encyclopedists. But after all, France and its people were still Catholic, even if this "eldest daughter of the Church" was pouting and rebellious, and even if its intellectual leaders were becoming skeptical and anticlerical.

But the American Union was a full-grown independent state, a completely heretical offspring, descended from a centuries-old family tree of heretics and apostates—Luther, Calvin, Zwingli, Henry VIII, De Molay, Elizabeth, John Smith, Wesley, and others.

America was an ever-stronger nation, built almost exclusively on Protestant principles and traditions, founded and molded in great part by leaders who drew their strength not only from their Protestant churches but from their fellowship and inspiration in that great supranational body which the Popes feared and hated so much —Freemasonry.

Centuries before, Pope Innocent III had excommuni-

### The Shot That Echoes Unceasingly

cated the English patriots who had forced King John to sign the Magna Carta in 1215. Papal fulminations would have been useless against George Washington, the Master of his Lodge, and the many Freemasons who had signed the Declaration of Independence of the colonies in 1776.

America was an ideological fortress, buttressed by beliefs and principles that were, at the time of its foundation and during the Civil War, as they remain today, the absolute antithesis of the dogmas and teachings upon which the continued existence and the future of the Church must depend.

The Roman Church continued to claim the Bible as its own private preserve, to be accepted as she alone interpreted it, while American Protestants encouraged every man to read the Sacred Book for himself and to worship God as he alone saw fit.

In 1865, America and its Protestant leadership, and particularly Lincoln, the Emancipator, were enemies. There could be no reconciliation of the authoritarianism of the Pope and the libertarianism of the President. Pius IX insisted, like his predecessors, that man *"sentire cum Ecclesia"* or "think with the Church," and that any speech, thought, or writing contrary to it must be crushed. American success, on the other hand, was based upon man's right to think for himself, with complete freedom of imagination, of initiative, of speaking, and of writing.

The Roman Hierarchy taught that it was the one, the only, and the true Church of Christ, and that every nation had the obligation to protect and support it. But America, vigorous new nation that it was, had cut all churches loose to fend for themselves. It had, in fact, erected a

## THE BACKGROUND

"wall of separation" between the Church and the State.

The Roman Church had never desired the education of the masses. It preferred their faithful illiteracy to skeptical literacy imbued with a spirit of doubting inquiry. Thus, while in Church-dominated lands education was reserved for the few and the rich, America was building schools for everyone, and while this nation was still young, had taken measures to compel all children to attend these schools.

The papacy drew its strength from the "divine right of kings," claiming that all ruling power was channeled through it, and that it alone could absolve whole nations of allegiance to their rulers. The leadership in America, however, taught that the right to govern arose only from the consent of the governed, and that the people alone could withdraw that right.

Protestant America, stronghold of Freemasonry, was not an ephemeral, petulant upheaval. It was a solid, growing, powerful nation, demonstrating to all peoples, including the Catholic-dominated countries of Europe and Latin America, that its principles of freedom of thought, speech, worship, and initiative brought strength, prosperity, and ample time for the pursuit of happiness.

To the alarm and chagrin of the Vatican, other countries were following the American rebellion and were defying the Church as well as their imperialist exploiters, the so-called mother countries. The priest, Hidalgo, threw away his cassock and, with the rallying cry of *grito* (or the cry of Dolores) led an army of Mexican people against their Church-supported Spanish oppressors. When

## The Shot That Echoes Unceasingly

the ecclesiastics had him shot in the summer of 1811, a fellow-priest, Morales, quit saying Mass and picked up the banner of his martyred comrade. He, too, was shot.

At the time of Lincoln, Benito Juarez, the full-blooded Mexican Indian, consummated the break with Spain and the Church. In the *Ley de la Reforma* of 1857, he confiscated the millions in land and buildings that the Hierarchy had garnered from the Indians and the Spaniards alike. Over the centuries, pious people had given them enough as *mandas* (votive offerings) or *limosnas* (alms) to appease or seduce long-dead virgins and saints, or had bequeathed enough property for masses for their souls, until the followers of poor Jesus owned most of the country.

Above all others, there had been Simon Bolivar, dynamic hero of the revolutionary Latin American struggles for independence. A Catholic and a Mason, Bolivar, during a visit to the United States, had been inspired in his revolutionary leadership by the impressions made on him by the free institutions that he witnessed, and he returned to Venezuela to lead the struggle against Spanish colonialism and ecclesiastical oppression.

With all Latin American countries gone from the control of Rome and of her puppets, with Catholic France kicking up her intellectual heels, with the Italian Catholic Mason, Garibaldi, together with his compatriots, Victor Emmanuel and Mazzini, whipping up the Italian people in large numbers to revise the Lord's Prayer to read: "Give us this day our daily ammunition and deliver us from the Austrians and the priests"—with all this, it is

## THE BACKGROUND

no wonder that uneasy rested the head that wore the tiara, and that the old Pope was getting emotionally crochetty and theologically dictatorial.

And Abraham Lincoln was the personification or the image of the great success of heresy, of everything this acrimonious Holy Father loathed and despised. He was the world's most eloquent spokesman for the principles that, could they long endure, would strip the Vatican of its power, its prestige, and its wealth, and could eventually relegate the papacy to its proper niche in the history of a bygone and never to be revived period, with the priesthoods of the Egyptians, Babylonians, Persians, Aztecs, and Incas.

The fear of what Lincoln typified was the strongest motive that the followers of Rome could have had for desiring and plotting his assassination. The entire Roman Hierarchy would be able to enjoy its siestas with tranquillity if the voice of the Great Emancipator were to be silenced by death.

Violent murder and imprisonment in dungeons had for more than a thousand years been the ultimate method utilized by the papacy for the elimination of dangerous religious and political opinions and for the silencing of competition. This is the principal reason why the popes themselves in earlier centuries reigned for only a few years, and frequently for but a few months. Catholic historians related how, in the ninth century of our era, members of the papal household killed Pope John VIII with a hammer "because poison was too slow."

The great contemporary historian, Will Durant, points out the almost unbelievable truth that the Vatican inquisitorial agents were far more ruthless than the pagan Roman emperors:

> The methods of the inquisitors, including torture, were adopted into the law codes of many governments; and perhaps our contemporary secret torture of suspects finds its model in the Inquisition even more than in Roman law. Compared with the persecution of heresy in Europe from 1227 to 1492, the persecution of Christians by Romans in the first three centuries after Christ was a mild and humane procedure. Making every allowance required of an historian and permitted to a Christian, we must rank the Inquisition, along with the wars and persecutions of our time, as among the darkest blots on the record of mankind, revealing a ferocity unknown in any beast.[2]

Finally, there were the ever-loyal and efficient Jesuits, with their vow of abject obedience to their Father General and the Pope.

The Jesuits, while they permitted the Dominicans to have the public laurels of heading the honor corps of the Inquisition, became the true cloak-and-dagger hatchet men of the Vatican—a deadly papal Mafia. John Hus, Savonarola, and Joan of Arc are merely the best known of the hosts of martyrs who were robbed, imprisoned or burned at the stake—not for murder, rape, horse-stealing, or crimes against the State—but merely because they were "heretics"—that is, extremely conscientious people who simply saw in the Word of God a meaning different from that taught by the pope.

Roman Catholic historians, when they acknowledge the historical existence of the Inquisition at all, paint it as a pious instrumentality of the Church designed to encourage doctrinal orthodoxy, but perverted by ultra-patriotic Spaniards into a lethal machine against their national enemies, the Moors and the Jews. They conveniently gloss over the barbarian cruelty of the pious priestly inquisitors in Italy, France, Germany, the Low Countries, England, and the Scandinavian lands.

There were no Moors and few Jews in Peru, where I saw the Hall of the Inquisition, the dungeons of imprisonment, and the gorgeously carved door with the hole in it—an opening made at mouth height so that the witness could testify against the accused heretic without being seen or identified, in a manner conforming to Church law and practice.

Thus, there were many motives behind the attitude of the Church toward the forcible removal of Lincoln. But the Jesuits provided the intellectual and theoretical leadership. A refinement of the Jesuit "Maxims of Life" provided for their anonymity by the use of paid assassins; again, this is an application of their guiding principle: "What is likely to bring disfavor, get others to do."

Furthermore, the moralistic members of the Society of Jesus could always quiet the conscience of one chosen to abduct or kill a heretic, by the thesis that the elimination of such an Enemy of the Faith or such a tyrant (as many Catholics in the United States, and not merely in the Confederacy, considered Abraham Lincoln to be) was not a sin at all. In fact, it was an act of virtue.

Let us, then, look for a moment into the line of theoretical reasoning that pervaded the Jesuit outlook.

Chapter Two

# The Theory That Justified the Act

The higher echelons of the Society of Jesus are so secret that even its members know little about them, while priests of other orders consider Jesuits the secret police of the Vatican. They are reluctant to talk about the "fourth vow." They will admit only that it is a second vow of absolute, complete and utter obedience to the pope and to the General of the Order. All members of all Catholic religious orders assume the customary three vows, which include obedience as well as poverty and chastity. Most Jesuits themselves do not know which of their fellows have taken this final vow, and it is well-nigh impossible to find out the wording of it.

But one is forced to pause and wonder what this vow might be, in the light of certain approved and acknowledged words included in the oath of obedience to the pope taken even in our own day by every Roman Catholic bishop in the world:

> With all my power I shall track down and attack all heretics, schismatics and those who rebel against the Lord Pope and his successors.[1]

## THE BACKGROUND

One of the moral puzzles of the Lincoln assassination plot is the conscience of Mary Surratt. As will be shown later, she was an extremely devout Roman Catholic. Yet of all the conspirators, she was the one who most persistently determined that Lincoln had to be eliminated. Vice-President Johnson called her home "the nest in which the egg was hatched." Yet, when the deed was done she felt no moral remorse. She spoke to her daughter, Anna, like a Prophet of the Old Testament, piously gloating over the destruction of Sodom and Gomorrah: "Booth was an instrument in the hands of the Almighty to punish this wicked and licentious people."

Mrs. Surratt was so completely indoctrinated by Catholic priests that their influence over her moral concepts can hardly be denied. They visited her house constantly. She corresponded with them. Her son studied to be one of them. Five priests testified at her trial and two accompanied her to the gallows.

Mrs. Surratt had been convinced that the killing of Abraham Lincoln was not a sinful crime. To her it was a good act of an avenging God.

The thought that priests of a Christian or any other religious order could condone murder, much less participate in a conspiracy to perpetrate murder, and still less, deliberately commit it themselves, is repugnant if not inconceivable to a modern American, be he Protestant or Catholic. A writer who would make such an insinuation, even as a possibility, would be certain to be branded as unhistorical and discredited, on the one hand, and if he be an ex-priest, as anti-Catholic and bitter, on the other.

### The Theory That Justified the Act

But the logical deductions of Catholic theology, as well as the explicit statements of the bolder theologians and the facts of history, are plain to any priest or Latin-speaking layman who dares to look beyond the sugar-coating of modern theologians, or the whitewashing of Church historians.

Greatest of all authorities and spokesmen of the Roman Catholic Church was St. Thomas Aquinas. His *Summa Theologica* is still the highest authoritative work of both dogmatic and moral theology. He stated very clearly that Catholics owed no obedience to non-Catholic rulers, and followers of St. Thomas, priests and laymen, could only interpret this as meaning that no allegiance was owed to a man like Abraham Lincoln.

Acclaimed by the Church as the "angelic doctor," St. Thomas Aquinas also taught that non-Catholics, or heretics, could, after a second warning, be legitimately killed. In fact, the exact words that he used are: *"they must be exterminated"* and (in verbatim translation) *"they have merited to be excluded from the earth by death."* [2]

Readers familiar with Latin may refer to the original: *Non modo excommunicationis sententia sed etiam saecularibus principibus exterminandi, tradendi sunt. . . . Meruerunt non solum ab Ecclesia per excommunicationem separari, sed etiam per mortem a mundo excludi.*[3]

Any priest, following the teachings of the greatest Catholic authority, would not find it difficult to believe in his own righteousness if he counseled that it was not only morally permissible to kill Abraham Lincoln, but more than that, it was morally advisable and desirable to do so.

## THE BACKGROUND

It is not difficult to imagine what fanatical followers, imbued with such theoretical support from so saintly a source, would do under such circumstances.

The theological legerdemain of "probabilism" would also enable a priest, especially a Jesuit, to condone the assassination of Abraham Lincoln—and even to encourage and to plot it. For it was in probabilism that the Church gave justification to those who might waver and might question the propriety of such acts as murder.

In its simplest form, probabilism is defined as a theory of Roman Catholic theology "that in cases of doubt as to the lawfulness or unlawfulness of an action, it is permissible to follow a soundly probable opinion favoring its lawfulness"! It is a theory that since its development has been associated within the Church primarily with the Jesuits.

Armed with the theory of probabilism, Catholic theologians found it possible to call an act murder in one generation and the same act a good deed in another.

For centuries, Catholic theologians have argued over the standards to be used in gauging the sinfulness and the degree of sinfulness (mortal or venial, sending the soul to hell or to purgatory) of many controversial actions. Such could be the fast before receiving communion, degrees of drunkenness, the amount necessary to make a theft serious, the morality of surgery in ectopic pregnancies, and countless other situations.

The evolution of moral "systems" or "methods" for the guidance of theologians, teachers, and priest-confessors did not occur until the end of the sixteenth century. It was at that time that Catholic morality evolved into its

## The Theory That Justified the Act

present recognizable form, and in the same century the Society of Jesus was founded.

In earlier principles that were used for moral guidance by the Church, the priest was obliged to advise his people to follow the opinion that was *more probably true*, for instance, that stealing fifty dollars was a mortal sin, punishable by hell fire, if not confessed. This theory of morality is called "probabiliorism" or sometimes "tutiorism" (more safe).

Some of these professors of morality followed a strict tightrope theory called "equiprobabilism." If the arguments for and against the morality of an action are about even, then it is no sin to perform it. A further refinement of this confusion is contained in "compensationism" which requires that before the action is permissible, it must also be useful. This theory would eliminate all dubious pleasant actions performed "just for the fun of it."

But "probabilism" was the key that opened Pandora's jar. It was the principle that could be used to justify anything the Church wanted to justify, from the assassination of a "tyrant" to stealing ("occult compensation"), from ectopic surgery to the rhythm method of birth control. That it has not been extended to cover abortion and routine methods of contraception, when its application is so obvious, can be explained only by the argument that the Church wants more babies: an increase of human population means an increase of Catholic population.

According to the Church dogma and its official interpretation, "probabilism" is a Roman Catholic system of morality that considers an action lawful and permissible just so long as there is a "reputable" teacher who says

## THE BACKGROUND

the action is "probably" lawful, even though the bulk or the majority of opinions are against it.[4]

For example, since the Jesuit Juan Mariana was a "reputable" and recognized moral theologian, and since he stated that the killing of an "unjust" king or ruler was legitimate and could be performed without any "due process," therefore the act would be considered just and sinless, even if all other theologians were against Mariana's view—which, incidentally, they were not!

Probabilism as a moral system was first propounded by a Dominican priest, Bartholomew Medina, in the sixteenth century. It was soon embraced enthusiastically by Jesuit leaders. The other religious orders fought it as being conducive to laxity and the breakdown of morality. When one Jesuit professor, Thyrsus Gonzalez, S. J., wrote a book against probabilism, in 1670, the General of the Order Oliva forbade its publication.[5]

The Jesuit adoption of probabilism is significant and very understandable. The Jesuits wanted power. They knew that the confessors of the princes and of their women could easily control them. That meant power. They knew also what every priest knows, that the more understanding, gentle, and tolerant the confessor is, the longer he remains the confessor and the greater power he can develop.

Probabilism gave the Jesuit priest a tremendous advantage over his more rigorous ecclesiastical colleagues.

An ancient secret Jesuit manual contains these words:

> In regard to the direction of the consciences of great men, we confessors must follow the writers who concede the

### The Theory That Justified the Act

> greater liberty of conscience. The contrary of this is to appear too religious; for that they will decide to leave others and submit entirely to our direction and counsels.[6]

When an opinion, such as the private personal killing of an undesirable ruler or tyrant, called regicide, is approved by only one or a few Catholic teachers, then it is merely "probable"—but under the Jesuit system, it is justifiable. When these teachers have convinced several others of the correctness of the act, then the opinion becomes "more probable" or "probabilior" and there can be no legitimate theological objection to it. This is what happened to the teaching on regicide.

Jesuit theological writers went much further than the shadowy, dubious liberties of probabilism in their sentiments regarding rulers who jeopardized their power or that of their patrons in the Vatican. Many specifically taught that "unjust tyrants" could be murdered, and that such an act of murder would not be sinful.

Among the many who advocated and defended the right and the righteousness of private assassination of a tyrant were the Jesuits Fr. Martin Becan, Fr. Paul Comitolo, Fr. Emmanuel Sa, Fr. Adam Tanner, Fr. Jean Gingnare, Fr. Juan Mariana, Fr. Carlos Scribanus, St. Robert Bellarmine, and Fr. Francisco Suarez. They taught that the assassination was proper, particularly if the victim (that is, the "tyrant") was a heretic, by which was meant a non-Catholic, and that it was a laudable and virtuous act that could be carried out "without waiting for the sentence or the order of any judge."

Fr. Juan Mariana's work, which contains his lengthy

## THE BACKGROUND

treatise on the killing of rulers, is entitled, "Concerning the King and his Education" (*De Rege et Regis Institutione*) and was published in 1599. The "imprimatur" or approval of the Jesuit Order was dated Madrid, December 2, 1598 and is worded:

> I, Stephan Hojeda, Visitator of the Society of Jesus for the Province of Toledo, give, under the power of special authority from our General, Claudius Acquaviva, permission that the three books, Concerning the King and his Education, written by Father John Mariana, of the same Society, may be published, because they have been previously sanctioned by learned and distinguished men of our Order.[7]

It has been reported that John Wilkes Booth, as he jumped from the presidential box to the stage of the Ford Theatre, cried out: "Sic semper tyrannis!" The words were clearly inspired by Catholic teachings.

The theological system and the intrigues of the Jesuits are important in evaluating any possible relationship between the Roman Catholic Church and the conspiracy that culminated in the assassination of Lincoln. At the time of Lincoln, as now, the Jesuits comprised most of the writers and educators in the Catholic Church. They wrote most of the text books used in all seminaries. They were also deeply involved in the imperial invasion of Mexico, engineered by their Catholic majesties, Napoleon III and Franz Joseph of Austria, with Pope Pius IX as their advisor and co-conspirator.

The Jesuits had owned a tremendous share of confiscated Church property in Mexico, and were very close

## The Theory That Justified the Act

to Pius IX in his fight against the Italian people over the unification of Italy.

It is no wonder, then, that the name of the Society of Jesus crops up repeatedly in the story of the assassination of Lincoln—in the expression of interest in the act that came from the headquarters in Rome, in the sympathies of Georgetown College priests and graduates, and in the presence of the Jesuits at the later Surratt trial. But, above all else, it was the Society of Jesus that laid the theoretical groundwork for this act for many centuries, with a group of theories so immoral and antilegal that they could only incite and justify those persons drifting into the conspiratorial web.

Chapter Three

# Backdrop for Treason

For many years, Catholic teachers, textbooks, magazines and newspapers have hammered away at the thesis that their American adherents, especially the Irish, have been the most loyal citizens in the nation. So effective has been this propaganda that not only do Catholics but even non-Catholics believe it.

The members of the Church are said to have volunteered their money and their military service in every national crisis, far in excess of their proportionate percentage in the population. Federal tax aid for parochial schools, it is argued, is justified by the support given to the government throughout our history, a support said to stem from the manner in which Catholic schools train better and more loyal citizens, who are therefore our best guarantee against the onslaught of communism.

Catholic publications are replete with self-serving declarations of the patriotism and the loyalty of their followers, as exemplified by the following Fourth of July statement:

## Backdrop for Treason

> A good Catholic must of necessity be a good American. Many Catholics have volunteered their services and given their lives in every war in which the United States has been involved in defense of its freedom and democratic principles. From the Revolutionary War to the present, Catholics have written in their own blood their indelible loyalty and fidelity to their country, the United States of America.[1]

Even when dealing with the Civil War, the Church-rooted historians find it possible to emphasize the loyalty of Catholics during those tragic years:

> Dreary days again would come to the Church in America, but there would be no basis for criticism of Catholic loyalty. The patriotism of the faithful had met the supreme test in battle and proved true and unyielding.[2]

And well might these authors speak of the loyalty of many Church members, for there can be no question of the heroism and fidelity of numerous American Catholics in all our wars, as well as in time of peace. Yet, one might well wonder if these brave men have known and understood what they were fighting for. The teachings of their Church emphatically deny the freedom of thought, of speech, of writing, and of worship that are the foundations of American democracy and American greatness.

Nevertheless, without disparaging the heroism of the Kellys, the Sullivans and the Kennedys, it must in sober truth be pointed out that not all of their American-domiciled ancestors have earned a niche in a patriotic hall of fame. There was, for example, the story of the San Patricios.

The very existence of the San Patricios, or the St.

Patricians, and their unique role in American history, is unknown to priests and to educated laymen, alike. Who were these men?

The San Patricios were Irish American Catholic soldiers who, in the war with Mexico, deserted the United States Army in 1846, went over to the Mexican side, and fought against their fellow-citizens.

The scheme that resulted in the desertion was hatched by the Mexican General Santa Anna. He hired an opportunistic Irish priest, Reverend Eugene McNamara, who infiltrated the American lines and convinced his co-religionists that their divinely chosen role was to fight by the side of their fellow-Catholics, the Mexicans, against the land-grabbing Protestant Yankees. Because of their Irish birth and ancestry, the Mexicans called their new-found allies the San Patricios, naming the regiment after the patron saint of Ireland.

The rebellious soldiers took part in the Battle of Buena Vista; they fought again at Monterey and in other battles, each time on the side of Mexico. And when the war was over, those who survived and were captured were imprisoned or executed by the American Army as deserters.[3]

Probably the greatest historian of the Mexican War has described the formation of this band:

> A party of deserters (mostly Irish) from the American army, which served at Monterey . . . became the nucleus of the "San Patricio" corps.[4]

And again, the same historian, in a later passage:

> An artillery company was made up from American deserters, mostly Irishmen, under the name of San Patricio.[5]

**Backdrop for Treason**

And when the Mexican government was reeling in defeat, these American deserters were indeed important to the cause that they had espoused:

> The government (of Mexico) itself decided that against an army represented by American deserters as more than 16,000 strong, fully equipped, shortly to be reinforced, and soon to advance, the city could not possibly be held; and the favorite plan of the administration, the most promising that could be devised, was to buy up Scott's Irish soldiers through the priest McNamara, recently conspicuous in California, and facilitate their desertion by having Santa Anna attack Puebla. Should this fail, submission and peace appear to have been deemed inevitable.[6]

An American soldier described the sentiments of the loyal troops:

> At that time the United States was appealed to and they moved the batteries from their ships of war and filled them with provisions for starving Ireland; and at this time, these men, deluded by priests of their faith to violate their oaths, ungratefully, in our own clothing and with our arms—at the battle of Cherubusco, near the City of Mexico—turned upon their former comrades and laid them low. It was impossible to estimate the feeling of our men. At one time muskets were thrown aside and simply with the bayonet alone in hand, we met the enemy and captured over sixty of these deserters. There came an armistice, and during that armistice they were duly tried by court-martial, and, at Miscoac, in the presence of both armies, we hung thirty-two in good order.[7]

As the flood of illiterate Roman Catholic immigrants swelled the population of Eastern cities, thoughtful Protestants worried about their lack of adaptability to the young Republic's democratic way of life. This was especially true of the Irish. Between 1840 and 1860 they constituted two-thirds of the 1,700,000 Roman Catholic immigrants arriving in America.[8]

Probably because of their hatred for the only civil government they had known, that of the English in Ireland, they were accustomed to welcome and recognize only the leadership of the Church, specifically embodied in their own Irish priests who had accompanied them to the United States. Their priests, too, hated the British and unfortunately transferred their own feelings of defiance to the Anglo-Saxon public officials of the American cities who, to compound their iniquity, were also Protestants.

This anti-Protestant sentiment of the Irish was appealed to by the priest McNamara, in order to seduce his followers to join the Mexican Army, which was itself Catholic in composition. The same appeal was later to be used during the Civil War by Southern recruiters in Ireland, and by Bishop Lynch of Charleston in his attempts to coax the Vatican to recognize the Confederacy.

The Protestant civil leaders were amazed and alarmed, not only at the emotional, riotous propensities of these Irish immigrants, but also at the almost absolute control held over them by their priests and bishops. The ecclesiastical officials had the power not only to sway their people to support established government, but also to defy it.

Samuel B. Morse, famous scholar and inventor of the telegraph, expressed a widespread fear held by the American citizenry as the tide of immigration rose in the 1830's:

## Backdrop for Treason

To any such inquirers, let me say, there are many ways in which a body organized as are the Catholics, and moving in concert, might disturb (to use the mildest term) the good order of the republic, and thus compel us to present to observing Europe the spectacle of republican anarchy. Who is not aware that a great portion of that stuff which composes a mob, ripe for riot or excess of any kind, and of which we have every week or two, a fresh example in some part of the country, is a Catholic population; and what makes it turbulent?

Ignorance, an ignorance which it is for the interest of its leaders not to enlighten; for enlighten a man and he will think for himself, and have some self-respect; he will understand the laws and know his interest in obeying them. Keep him in ignorance, and he is the slave of the man who will flatter his passions and appetites, or awe him by superstitious fears. Against the outbreakings of such men, society, as it is constituted on our free system, can protect itself only in one of two ways: it must either bring these men under the influence and control of a sound republican and religious education, or it must call in the aid of the priests who govern them, and who may permit, and direct, or restrain their turbulence, in accordance with what they may judge at any particular time to be the interest of the church. Yes, be it well remarked, the same hands that can, whenever it suits their interest, restrain, can also, at the proper time, "let slip the dogs of war."

In this mode of restraint by a police of priests, by substituting the ecclesiastical for the civil power, the priest-led mobs of Portugal and Spain, and South America, are instructive examples. We have had riots again and again which neither the civil nor military power have availed anything to quell, until the magic 'peace, be still' of the Catholic priest has hushed the winds, and calmed the waves of popular tumult.

> While I write, what mean the negotiations, between the two Irish bands of emigrants, in hostile array against each other, shedding each other's blood upon our soil, settling with the bayonet miserable foreign feuds which they have brought over the waters with them?[9]

In Morse's day, the frequent riots among workers on the railroads, canals, and other public works were attributed to foreign immigrants. He quotes an example from the *Journal of Commerce* that illustrates the disregard of civil authority by the Irish Catholics and their docile subjection to the will of their priests:

> THE RIOTERS.—It appears by the following notice that the rioters on the Baltimore and Washington Rail-road have concluded a treaty of peace, through the intervention of a priest. There was considerable talk during the late riots in this city of calling in the agency of the priests, to put an end to the disturbance. No doubt it would have been effectual.

### AGREEMENT

> On the 24th of June, 1834, the subscribers, in the presence of the Rev. John McElroy, have respectively and mutually agreed to bury forever, on their own part, and on behalf of their respective sections of country, all remembrance of feuds and animosities, as well as injuries sustained. They also promise to each other, and make a sincere tender of their intention to preserve peace, harmony and good feeling between persons of every part of their native country without distinction.
>
> They further mutually agree to exclude from their houses and premises all disorderly persons of every kind, and par-

ticularly habitual drunkards. They are also resolved, and do intend to apply in all cases where it is necessary, to the civil authorities, or to the laws of the country for redress—and finally they are determined to use their utmost endeavors to enforce, by word and example, these, their joint and unanimous resolutions.

on behalf of all employed
Signed by fourteen of the men )
employed on the 4th, 5th and )
8th sections of the 2d division, )
B. and W. R. R. )
And also by thirteen of the 9th )
section of the 1st division.[10] )

The position of the Hierarchy was that it need not be bound by American civil law. If this meant disloyalty to the government, it was, the Church reasoned with arrogance and presumption, loyalty to a higher law, as interpreted by itself. Thus, in 1864, the State Constitution of Missouri was amended to require that all clergymen take an oath of loyalty to the State of Missouri and therefore to the United States.

At this crucial moment in the Civil War, the Roman Catholic archbishop of St. Louis sent a pastoral letter to all his priests condemning the required oath. He encouraged them to defy the government by telling them that if the civil authorities should try to force them to swear loyalty, they should inform him "of the particular circumstances of their position, in order that he might be able to give them council and assistance." Several priests refused to take the oath and were arrested.[11]

But before this, in July of 1863, what Samuel Morse had feared some two decades earlier actually took place.

There was a full-scale riot against the Government of the United States, a riot participated in almost exclusively by the Irish Catholics of New York City.

No Roman Catholic history text that I ever saw, in twenty-two years of association with parochial schools, has ever mentioned the Draft Riots of New York in 1863, much less their serious threat to the Union cause during the Civil War. We were taught, as the Catholic press so unctuously keeps repeating, for the general consumption of the faithful, that Catholic Americans have always been the loyal backbone of the nation—at all times, in peace and in war.

Yet, Leonard Patrick O'Connor Wibberley, historian and apologist for the Irish Catholics in America, admits that before the Civil War broke out, this group was very noisily and very openly against Lincoln and for the continuation of slavery.[12]

Held in a state of illiteracy in their Church-dominated homeland, sheltered from the liberal thinking of such American leaders as Emerson and Thoreau whom their leaders denounced as heretics, these men and women were unable to grasp the sociological significance of slavery as an institution, and they were too narrow and ritualistic in their simple faith to know of the "mystical body of Christ" or to understand the concept that, before God, all human beings had equal status.

Thus Wibberley wrote, only recently:

> Up to the moment that Beauregard opened fire on Fort Sumter, the Irish in America had been proslavery and inimical to Abraham Lincoln and the new Republican party.[13]

Exploited themselves, the Irish in America, gathered particularly in the burgeoning rural centers, knew only that they were the lowest paid and the most menial laborers, surrounded by a wealth that they could not share.

They deeply resented the freed Negroes who migrated northward and competed with them in the mills, in the ditches, and on the railroad tracks. What little economic security they had would be ruined, they felt, by the abolition of slavery. Any politician who wanted to free the slaves was a foe of the Irish Catholics—and that meant Lincoln most of all. In the words of Wibberley:

> On the continued bondage of the Negro depended the salvation of the Irish. That was the laborer's view. Anyone who wished to liberate the slaves was no friend of the Irish.[14]

When the South seceded from the Union and there began the War Between the States, the Emancipation Proclamation had not yet been issued. The Irish Catholics, mainly in the North, had before them several inducements for joining the Union forces.

For example, there were persistent rumors that England would side with the South, so that the Irish could achieve a long-repressed revenge by defeating an ally and friend of a traditional enemy. Then, too, there was money in fighting. The bounties offered for enlistment amounted to more than a year's pay for most Irishmen. This could be greatly multiplied by deserting and re-enlisting. Two Irishmen, Big Danny O'Brien and Mike Garrity, were persevering. Garrity, when finally caught, had enlisted and deserted no less than a dozen times.

This explanation of the recruiting, given by an Irish Catholic author, would seem to substantiate the circulated figures of the astounding number of desertions by Irish Catholics during the Civil War. Although only 9 per cent of the enlistees in the North (144,221) were Irish Catholics, fully 72 per cent of all deserters (104,000) were from this group. These figures and the percentages are readily understandable in the light of Wibberley's explanation that many of the emigrants from Ireland and their sons made a continuing profitable financial venture out of desertion.[15]

Furthermore, fighting in the Civil War provided military training to the Irish-Americans for that war which, to them, was really important, their dream of an invasion of England that would result in the liberation of the native land to which they still swore loyalty.

I can still remember the frenzied Irish patriotism of my own relatives. The contrast between their Sinn Fenian hatred of everything and everybody British with the love and charity presumably instilled by St. Patrick and his successors bothered them not a whit. We were released from parochial school to hear the sister of Eamon de Valera harangue the California State Legislature on her bond-selling trip to finance the war with England.

But we were never told, nor did our history books divulge, the story of the attempted invasion of England via Canada by Irish-Americans under the leadership of John O'Mahoney, "Fighting Tom" Sweeney, and General John O'Neill, shortly after the Civil War. Although the

### Backdrop for Treason

original plan was to launch the invasion of England directly from New York City, wiser and more sober leaders persuaded them that it would be simpler to conquer Canada first and then jump off from there.

These devotees of the Irish cause, although American residents and citizens, did not hesitate to show their allegiance to be elsewhere. They placed aside any loyalty to the United States, which today they would like to claim, and took an oath that read:

> I, —————, in the presence of Almighty God, do solemnly swear allegiance to the Irish Republic, now virtually established, and that I will do my utmost, at every risk, while life lasts, to defend its independence and integrity; and finally that I will yield implicit obedience in all things, not contrary to the law of God, to the commands of my superior officers. So help me God. Amen.[16]

Unmentioned in the history books, untaught in the schools, unknown to the present generation of Americans, the invasion of Canada did actually take place in 1866. Volunteers converged on Buffalo from Boston, New York, Louisville, Nashville, Chicago, St. Louis, Philadelphia, Cleveland, and Cincinnati.

The Irish of San Francisco sent a solid gold brick to help with the financing of the invasion. But it was to no avail. For Canada called out its militia to repel the invaders, and the ridiculous episode was brought to its abrupt termination when the American authorities, acting on orders of President Johnson, captured the whole of O'Neill's army.[17]

But before and during the Civil War, the Catholics in

the Southern States were even more ardently in favor of the continuation of slavery than were their Northern co-religionists. This was true even of the better educated, who could not have feared the freed Negroes as an economic threat to their security.

Modern writers, in boasting of the participation of Catholics in the Civil War, unwittingly expose this disloyalty of their religious ancestors. The Jesuit-controlled Georgetown University, oldest Catholic college in the United States, had 1500 graduates and students of military age in 1861. Of these, 951 joined the armies of the Confederacy, while only 210 were loyal to the American government.[18]

That this Roman Catholic disloyalty to the Union was endorsed by their Jesuit priests and by other Catholic priests is pointed up by the very famous Southern General, Stonewall Jackson, who apparently had many sympathetic confidants among the Catholic priests in the North. He inadvertently revealed this contact when discussing his attempts to locate the Union General, Jonathan P. Banks: "I will see what can be effected through the Catholic priests in Martinsburg." [18a]

Martinsburg, West Virginia, and Martinsburg, Pennsylvania were both in the North. Stonewall Jackson had become quite friendly with high Catholic officials when he was garrisoned in Mexico City after the War with Mexico. He had studied Catholicism under Archbishop Irisarri and had seriously considered joining the Church.[18b]

Yet, a few Irish Catholics were willing to fight in the Northern cause, so long as they received bounties for enlisting. But enlistments were insufficient to build the

**Backdrop for Treason**

forces necessary to crush the Southern rebellion. A National Draft Law was ordered into effect in July, 1863, only a few months after the issuance of the Emancipation Proclamation.

The Draft Law was resented by the immigrant population in the North. It was reminiscent of the forced military service in the European armies, from which many had fled. And it contained a provision whereby the wealthier classes could escape service either by hiring a substitute or by paying three hundred dollars to the government. Very few immigrant workingmen could afford to escape by either of these clauses.

The actual drafting of men in New York City was scheduled to begin on Monday, July 13, 1863. All Sunday afternoon the Irish jammed the bars of the East Side and the headquarters of the volunteer fire companies. Their mob anger mounted as their liquor vanished.

When the provost marshall started drawing names at 10 o'clock on Monday morning, the worst riot in American history broke loose. Shooting started. Paving stones and brickbats came flying through the windows. Kerosene was dumped over the floor, and the Government office was set afire.[19]

As word spread of the defiance to the Government, the crowd grew, until some fifty thousand, practically all Irish Catholics, took over the city. They looted the liquor stores, and then started on their siege of crime. Telegraph lines were torn down to disrupt police communications. The homes of the rich on Lexington Avenue were ransacked. Clothing and grocery stores were robbed and countless buildings were set on fire.

## THE BACKGROUND

The fury of the lawless mob was especially concentrated on Negroes. The barbaric manner in which the mobsters tracked down Negroes, tortured them, and slaughtered them is reminiscent only of the cruelest days of lynching parties in the South—episodes which the Church would piously condemn in later years.

With the usual cowardice characteristic of a mob, the group concentrated its fury on the orphan asylum for colored children, located on Fifth Avenue, between 43rd and 44th Streets. They set fire to different parts of the building in an attempt to burn the two hundred and thirty-three children alive. Some two thousand Irish men and women (for, according to eyewitness reporters, many women were in the crowd) milled around and through the building, shouting: "Murder the damned monkeys" and "Wring the necks of the damned Lincolnites." [20]

All over New York, the Negroes were pursued. If caught, a colored man was pounded to death. If he escaped into a house, it was set on fire and everyone in it burned to death. As reported by the greatest historian of this tragic episode:

> Deeds were done and sights witnessed that one would not have dreamed of except among savage tribes. At one time there lay at the corner of 27th Street and Seventh Avenue the dead body of a Negro, stripped nearly naked, and around it a collection of Irishmen, absolutely dancing and shouting like wild Indians. . . . It was a strange sight to see a hundred Irishmen pour along the streets after a poor Negro. [21]

The newspapers of the time and the court records as well point up shameful details of the orgy. A magistrate, one Judge Welsh, sat in court to try some of the captured rioters. As reported in *The New York Daily Tribune,* an abused woman testified:

> These men came to my house, and one of them, advancing to the table, struck it a rap with a heavy club which he carried and asked, "Do you know what we come for?" She replied, "I do not." "Do you know the Constitution?" "No." "Well," said the ruffian, "I will tell you; it is to rip and tear and carry off the niggers' property and kill the damned niggers." [22]

Two of the prisoners taken in the riot of Wednesday, July 15th, were mounted on a wagon while giving lusty cheers for Jefferson Davis. "In one instance," reported *The Tribune,* "the crowd in attacking a house used as their watchword: 'Burn out the heretics.'" [23]

"On Wednesday night a suspicious person was arrested on whom were found two pocketbooks, one containing some $600 in Confederate money and the other filled with greenbacks," reported *The Tribune,* while under the heading of "Fiendishness of the Rioters," it gave this harrowing report:

> A funeral procession was passing down Second Avenue on Tuesday last, and when near 19th Street it was stopped by a gang of rioters, who ordered the driver of the hearse to turn back. He expostulated with them, telling them that he had a corpse in the hearse. "Throw the corpse in the street," cried the ruffians, and suiting the action to the words they seized the coffin, pitched it into the street, and compelled the hearse and carriage drivers to flee for their lives. The father of the deceased and one or two of his friends returned to the spot at great risk, picked up the coffin, which was

SACKING A DRUG STORE IN SECOND AVENUE

HANGING A NEGRO IN CLARKSON STREET

### Backdrop for Treason

lying in the gutter, and carried it to a place of safety. The corpse remained unburied till yesterday. For the sake of human nature, we would gladly be spared the pain of recording these atrocities.[24]

Many members of the police force and, later in that gruesome week, soldiers too, were wounded, beaten, and killed by the mob. A reporter for *Harper's Weekly* described a scene that he had witnessed:

He (a New York Cavalry sergeant) was killed by a bullet fired from one of the houses in the vicinity, and then barbarously beaten and mangled by the mob. As he lay there, with a cloth thrown by some decent person over his face to hide his ghastly wounds, ill-looking women came now and then to look at him, jesting over the unconscious remains, and pointing them out to their infant children with fiendish glee. The little boys amused themselves by lifting up his hands, and then letting them fall to the ground with heavy "thud." Others performed savage dances around the body, jumping round it, and over it, and even upon it.[25]

The riot, with its hangings, beatings, pillaging and arson continued unchecked through July 13th, 14th, and 15th. Only two forces could subdue the mob: the Roman Catholic Church and the United States Army. But the Church would do nothing, and the Army had left New York City.

Historically, these acts of treachery to the Union cause are seen in perspective only when it is understood that they took place but a few days after the Battle of Gettysburg. One of the saddest moments in American history, where men had fallen "on hallowed ground," all available

CHARGE OF THE POLICE ON THE RIOTERS AT THE "TRIBUNE" OFFICE

### Backdrop for Treason

troops had been rushed to the Pennsylvania township to bolster the bitterly assaulted Union lines. New York City itself was left with only its brave but all too small police force—a force that had never been organized or trained to cope with a mob of 50,000 frenzied men and women, many intoxicated, all lawless and out of control.

Vital as was the battle taking place in Gettysburg, the United States Army nevertheless was compelled to rush many soldiers to New York in order to crush the treacherous outbreak of the rioters. New York officials, grasping the significance of the religious issue, asked that Protestant soldiers be sent.

Thus, nine New York regiments and one from Michigan, all loyal American Union troops, deployed from the battle against the Confederate secessionists, were finally able to restore order in the city. The mopping up operations were completed by Thursday, July 16th.

Order having been restored, the rioters now subdued and defeated, innocent lives having been lost in murder, arson, and pillage, Archbishop John Hughes finally stepped into the picture. Tranquility once more prevailed. Law had triumphed. The crisis was ended.

Catholic historians, in their effort to sift the ashes of the past for examples of loyalty and heroism among their adherents, always cite the name of Archbishop John Hughes of New York City. He is mentioned as a great patriot who travelled in Europe as Abraham Lincoln's representative and who secured the "neutrality" of Napoleon III of France. He also allegedly forestalled Pope Pius IX's official recognition of the Confederacy.

During the entire course of the Draft Riots, the Archbishop had been in New York. Catholic historians depict him as a sickly, pathetic, broken man who, in response to the plea of Governor Seymour, crawled to his porch and from his chair of pain begged his Irish faithful to quit their murder and their plunder and go back to work. He returned to his sick bed and, these historians state, he died six months later.[26]

The historical facts present a totally different picture of the good Archbishop's loyalty and courage, and of the efforts that he made (or failed to make) in order to stop the riot. That he could have stepped in and stopped it on the first day, there is no doubt, for it was almost exclusively a mob made up of his followers.

Priests moved at will, and safely, among the rioters. A city official, one Mr. Crowley, trying to repair cut telegraph lines, was afraid to risk the mob until he saw a passing carriage containing a Catholic priest. He got into the carriage, and as it approached the mob, the carriage was surrounded by ruffians. The latter, thinking at first that the passengers were members of the press, shouted, "Down with the reporters." But when they recognized the priest, they became quiet and let the carriage pass.[27]

Many writers of the time felt that the New York riot was a deliberately incited act of treason, designed to mesh with riots, arson, and poisoning attempts in other Northern cities, in order to subdue the Northern will to fight on. It was a conspiracy, they contend, that would lead to a victory of the Confederacy. In this effort, Archbishop Hughes can only be viewed as an accessory to the scheme, an unwitting ally, who was unwilling to use his prestige, power, and influence to sway his Irish followers.

### Backdrop for Treason

Archbishop Hughes showed no will or desire to restrain his people. He finally spoke to them—after remaining silent throughout the riots. When did he break his silence? The day *after* the Army had returned to New York and had successfully put an end to the riot by the use of military force!

To the rioters themselves, during the height of their lawlessness, he was silent. It required no courage to come before them after they had been quieted and disarmed. But finally he spoke up, and when he did, what did the Archbishop have to say? His speech was nothing more than a satirical post mortem, a fitting epitaph to his days of silence.

During the riot, this feeble patriot had spent his days composing a vitriolic letter of some 3,000 words damning Horace Greeley. On the last day of the violence, Thursday the 16th of July, Greeley published this historic document. It is a letter that can only be described as a justification of the riot and as further inciting the mob to continue their plunder.[28]

But when, on the following day, the riot was over, the Archbishop addressed the multitude. A Catholic-trained, self-willed and determined young widow had forced her way into his office early in the week and had demanded that he recognize his responsibility and do something to stop the Irish Catholic lawlessness. But his silence was to be broken only when the riot had been stopped by other voices and other hands.

The Archbishop's speech was printed verbatim in *The Tribune* on Saturday, July 18th. His sarcasm, satire and attempted wit belie both his feebleness and his loyalty:

FIGHT BETWEEN RIOTERS AND MILITARY

RUINS OF THE PROVOST-MARSHAL'S OFFICE

**Backdrop for Treason**

Men of New York: They call you rioters, but I cannot see a riotous face among you. (cheers) I will call you Men of New York; not gentlemen, because 'gentlemen' is so threadbare a term that it means nothing positive. (laughter) Give me men, for I know of my own knowledge that if this city were invaded by a British or any foreign power the delicate ladies of New York, with infants on their breasts, would look for their protection more from men than from gentlemen. (laughter and applause) . . . If you are Irishmen—for your enemies say the rioters are Irishmen—I am also an Irishman, but not a rioter. (silence) If you are Catholics, as they have reported —probably to hurt my feelings—then I am a Catholic, too. (cheers) . . . In Europe, where the countries call themselves constitutional, a fool or a wise man must occupy the throne, and there is nothing for an oppressed people but you as the President (derisive laughter) or as the Mayor, or as a military officer. I address you as your father; and I am not going into a question of what has brought about this unhappy state of things. It is not my business for I am a minister of God. You know I have never deserted you. (Never, Never cheers) . . . Revolution is a terrible thing. But in this country the country gives the right to the people to make a revolution every four years. (cheers) . . . I am too old now to go to another country. I want the housekeeps to mind. (laughter—a voice 'Let the Niggers keep South') . . . In case of a violent and unjust assault on you without provocation—my notion is that every man has a right to defend his house or his shanty at the risk of life. ('That's so'—great cheering) . . . You have suffered already. No government can save itself unless it protects its citizens. Military force will be let loose upon you. The innocent will be shot down and the guilty will be likely to escape. Would it not be better for you to retire quietly. I do not ask you to give up your principles or convictions. (Applause) [29]

Here was the soft slap on the wrist that Catholic historians have pointed to as proof of the Archbishop's loyalty to Lincoln and the Union. An editorial in *Harper's Weekly* called it "blarney" and added:

> Through all the long speech of the Archbishop we look in vain for the tone of indignant reproof, or the plain command of Jesus. My sweet good masters, he says in effect, if indeed you have been naughty—and I'm sure you do not look as if you were so—please be good boys, or you will make me feel very unpleasant. I am sure you will be good, because your countrymen have always been the most innocent of babes. Go home then, like good children—Amen! [30]

Draft riots occurred in other cities. But the riot of New York stands out because it was so vicious, came so close to damaging the Union cause, and resulted in the death of so many people.

The power of the Hierarchy over the ignorant immigrants and their children has been demonstrated on countless occasions. But the riots proved the disregard of the Hierarchy toward murder, arson, and wholesale pillage. When it was not good politics and timely to condemn such acts, the Church remained silent and even condoned them. But above all, the riots proved the disloyalty of the Irish Catholics, their priests and their Hierarchy, toward the cause of the Union at a juncture of the Civil War when the preservation of the nation hung in its most precarious balance.

If the Roman Catholic Church, in the action (or lack of action) of its most vaunted leader did so little to help the nation survive, why should anyone be surprised if it followed through in its sympathy for the Confederacy and had a hand in the plot to kill the Union's most beloved leader? When it condoned all the murders in New York, why should it hesitate in being a party to the plot to assassinate the President against whose policies these murders were directed?

Chapter Four

# Conspiracy South of the Border

It is impossible to grasp the relationship between Rome and Washington, Vatican and Presidency, ecclesiastical power and secular strength, without viewing what was taking place South of the Rio Grande.

The ultimate aims of their Catholic Apostolic Majesties, including the conniving empresses and Pope Pius IX, as well as his Secretary of State Cardinal Antonelli, were summarized by the historian, A. R. Turner-Tyrnauer:

> (1) The occupation of Mexico for the new imperial regime; (2) overt financial and moral—and clandestine military—support of the Confederacy; (3) recognition of the Confederate states at an opportune moment; (4) gradual re-introduction of the monarchic system of government into a divided United States; (5) suppression of all republican regimes and revolutions in the New World.[1]

In early 1865, when Union victory finally seemed inevitable, even the Confederate leaders themselves seemed to prefer absorption by Europe to surrender to Lincoln. On January 6, 1865, Chevalier Carl F. von Loosey, Aus-

## Conspiracy South of the Border

trian Consul General in New York, sent to Emperor Franz Joseph an article from the *Richmond Sentinel* which was attributed to Jefferson Davis himself:

> We lately published . . . a suggestion that, in the event of being unable to sustain our independence, we should surrender it into the hands of those from whom we wrested or purchased it, into the hands of Britain, France and Spain, rather than yield it to the Yankees.
>
> From the favor with which this suggestion has been received, we are sure that in the dread event which it contemplates, our people would infinitely prefer an alliance with European nations on terms as favorable as they could desire, in preference to the domination of the Yankees.[2]

The insoluble incompatibility between traditional Vatican theological intolerance, on the one hand, and the naive openhearted tolerance of all religions in the United States, on the other, is shown in the Vatican involvement in Latin America at the time of Abraham Lincoln and our War Between the States.

Most Americans, both in school and as adult citizens, think of the American stage, with its Civil War, its political struggles, its central figure of Lincoln, all as an isolated theatrical production of the mid-nineteenth century. We are apt to forget that the United States, with its fight for survival, occupied only one ring in this contemporary circus of history.

It was, indeed, a many-ringed circus. Simultaneously, but in other rings, playing before the audience of the world, there was France, at whose head was Napoleon III, assuming the trappings of empire to cover the obscurity of his beginnings.

In the ring of Austria there was Emperor Franz Joseph, acting as the front-man barker, distracting the sightseers, while Metternich and the mentally poor relations of the House of Hapsburg connived in the shadows to uphold and strengthen the family fortunes.

The Italians, figuratively then as many are in reality today, were trapeze artists. Garibaldi, Mazzini, Cavour, and King Victor Emmanuel were flying all over the tent, needling the French armies, dodging the Austrian forces, grabbing duchies and provinces, as they worked inexorably and hacked away at the Papal States for the unification of Italy.

At the same time, the British plied their trade in the reserved seats and the bleachers, avoiding the spotlight, selling their wares and munitions as usual to all buyers —the South in the United States, the rebels in Mexico, the armies in Italy, while threatening to foreclose on those purchasers who, like Mexico, failed to pay on time. In a ring at the far end, out of range of the main spotlights, was Latin America—boiling, fighting, erupting, seething, declaring independence, confiscating churches, killing and deporting priests and bishops.

But, to complete the figure of speech, outside the big top, like a deposed ringmaster hiding in an office under the grandstand, was the entrepreneur who had pulled the strings and called the signals in all the circus rings, gathering the treasures and the riches before the sheriff or the gangsters might arrive: this was Pius IX.

The foreign situation contemporaneous with Lincoln

that best points up the complete and irreconcilable incompatibility between the principles of freedom for which Abraham Lincoln fought and died, and the unyielding mental, financial and military tyranny of Catholicism and its Papal leader, is that which was taking shape on our doorstep.

Here in Mexico was a great democratic leader, Benito Juarez, freeing his people from peonage and actual literal bondage to the Catholic Church, by restoring its stolen property to the nation and declaring men free to think, speak, read and worship in complete freedom—the identical principles that were guiding the neighbor to the North, the Unted States.

The Jesuits and the bishops, with so much wealth at stake from their self-gorging through the centuries, were not content to fight for their "rights," politically and legally. In order to discredit the democratic Juarez regime abroad, especially in England, France, Spain and Austria, these avowed followers of the Prince of Peace unleashed and directed a guerrilla warfare of pillage, brigandage, torture, and murder that brought chaos into their own country.

These treacherous priests and bishops deliberately ruined their own country, while their archbishop, exiled to Europe, plotted wth Napoleon III, Franz Joseph, and Pope Pius IX to usurp the sovereignty of Mexico, to send in a conquering French army, and place Emperor Maximilian on a throne—all to regain the property of Mexico and to stifle again the intellectual freedom of its people.

It was this Pope and his ecclesiastical brethren—with consecrated hands dripping with the blood not of Christ

## THE BACKGROUND

in their sacrifice of the Mass, but with the very real blood of their own members and fellow-citizens in Mexico (and during the same years in the Papal States in Italy)—these were the men who would not hesitate to conspire and plot the overthrow and forcible removal of one more man, Abraham Lincoln.

The Catholic-directed, inspired, and supported murders and assassinations in Mexico, that took place while Lincoln was the occupant of the White House, are evidence of how far Rome would go to salvage a few millions in property and gold-dripping altars, and to keep Indian and mestizo peons from thinking for themselves and joining Protestant denominations.

With an easy conscience, Rome could go much further than she had done in the U.S.A. before, in order to forestall the growth and expansion of that greater enemy —democracy. It was democracy, with its freedom of thought, and particularly freedom of religion, that threatened the security of the Vatican. This was the force that was feared. This was the idea which, if permitted to spread, could destroy the Vatican's influence, its wealth, and its power.

When a nation, once torn asunder and now reunited, felt that its hope for the enduring of those ideals of freedom were incarnated in one man, it was fitting that he should be removed. This was a trivial peccadillo to commit for the elimination of so great a threat.

Meanwhile, South of the border, Mexico was being torn by the Vatican-Napoleon-Austrian conspiracy. Contemporaneous with Abraham Lincoln and with our Civil

War, and on our very doorstep, the Vatican was shamelessly displaying its contempt for a government representative of the people. It was demonstrating its willingness to use any means—pillage, assassination and military conquest—in violation of all national rights, in order to achieve wealth and power. It is a story voluminously and incontestably documented.

By the midyears of the nineteenth century, the Roman Catholic Church had been in Mexico, as in all other Latin American countries, for some three hundred and fifty years. Catholicism was the state religion, the sole Christianizing, civilizing, educational and moral force.

The educational program of the Church in Latin America, as elsewhere, consisted in teaching the children of the rich proper manners and the glory of the imperial power (mainly Spain) and of the Church, while spreading a veneer of Catholic ritual over the pagan beliefs of the enslaved Indians and peons. Literacy, the ability to read and write, was neither necessary nor desirable for the masses.

As generations were born and died, countless Mexican souls crowded into Purgatory. Prayers and Masses were the most effective means of relieving that congestion of the netherworld. Families, the grandees and the peons, gave their money and willed their property to the Church as memorials, for novenas, for anniversary Masses, and for the perpetual remembrances for themselves and their relatives.

After three hundred years, the wealth of the Roman Catholic Church in poor, sparsely populated and underdeveloped Mexico was between $250,000,000 and $300,-000,000—a fabulous fortune today, and even more staggering as wealth was computed a century ago.[3]

The Church owned from one-third to one-half of all the land of the nation. Its revenues from tithes, Masses, and the sale of devotional articles such as statues, medals, rosaries, and the like, amounted to between six and eight million dollars annually, while its total revenues reached the astronomical figure of twenty million dollars.

The magnitude of this wealth can be realized by a comparison. This drain on the poor country of Mexico was equal to the operating expense of the entire United States Government during these same years.

The most intolerable financial oppression existed in the capital city itself. As stated by one authoritative source:

> One-half of all the property of the City of Mexico, including many millions in money, is in the hands of the Archbishop, who thereby wields a power unknown to other countries and does not disdain to assume the function of a banker.[4]

The oppression by Spain and the oppression by the Church of Rome were so intermeshed as to be indistinguishable by the people. The Hierarchy supported the Spanish regime and excommunicated, through its New World Inquisition, anyone resisting the power of the state, just as it did all religious doctrinal heretics. The government in turn enforced Church laws and, as the "secular arm," functioned as disciplinarian and even as executioner for the Church.

Finally, in 1861, the year that Abraham Lincoln entered the White House, Benito Juarez, full-blooded Indian and

## Conspiracy South of the Border

greatest hero of Mexico, marched into Mexico City with his army.

The similarity between the two leaders who now occupied the position of titular and popular heads of their neighboring countries is almost providentially coincidental. Both were from the humblest origins. Both were self-made men and leaders. Both hated tyranny and passionately loved freedom.

South of the border the Indian was doing as much that "freedom might long endure" as the railsplitter was doing in the States. Lincoln issued the Emancipation Proclamation to free the slaves of America. Juarez proclaimed the *Ley de la Reforma* (the Law of Reform) to free the slaves of Mexico. Both men were loved by their peoples, and both were deeply and thoroughly hated by enemies within their countries.

Each of the two national leaders and heroes showed himself to be aware of the ideological comradeship of the other. In early 1861, Juarez sent his representative, Matias Romero, to Springfield to congratulate Lincoln upon his election. Lincoln in turn appointed a friend of Juarez, Thomas Corwin, as American minister to Mexico.[5]

Particularly, however, was the bond of friendship between the two men demonstrated when Lincoln consistently refused to recognize the regime that deposed Juarez, and when Juarez a short time later was to express deep and warm sympathy to America upon the tragic loss of her leader through the bullet of an assassin.[6]

The strongest provisions of the Law of Reform, frequently referred to as the Mexican declaration of independence, were directed against the Roman Catholic

Church. Complete freedom of worship was granted. The Catholic Church was disestablished and disendowed. All Catholic Church property, including rectories, convents, shrines, churches, basilicas, and cathedrals, were confiscated.[7]

The plutocratic Archbishop of Mexico City and five other bishops were thrown out of the country for resisting the decrees. As the Hierarchy had done for centuries, they scurried to the Pope for protection. From the safety of the Vatican they launched their customary ecclesiastical anathemas.

On December 26, 1863, the Mexican Hierarchy formally excommunicated Juarez and everyone else involved in the struggle he was leading, which included the bulk of thinking Mexicans, and stated that:

> They cannot be absolved, not even at the point of death, if they do not comply with the conditions established by the Church, and set forth in our circulars and diocesan decrees aforesaid.[8]

The excommunications against Juarez and other leaders of the Mexican struggle for independence were mere ecclesiastical trappings. The realistic Hierarchy was made of sterner stuff. The melodramatic struggle to recoup lost wealth and power would bar no holds, as witness these eloquent words of a recent historian:

> There are to be cloaks and swords in plenty, a hero highborn and comely, lovely women—one of the loveliest of her age—conspiratorial whisperings, noises of battle off-stage, the Church's blessing, parental counsel, an Emperor to pledge

his honor, a throne to be won far away in the West, and at the end—madness, ruin and death.[9]

The frontmen for the Hierarchy amongst the laymen were a triumvirate of Mexican exiles—General Almonte, Jose Hidalgo, and their leader Maris Gutierrez de Estrada. This latter gentleman, always impeccably groomed and elegant in appearance, had been born and reared in Mexico to the enjoyment, not the production, of wealth. Like most of his caste he had been educated by the Jesuits, and like his teachers he felt and preached that Mexico could be stabilized only by an "Absolute and Catholic Monarchy."

With this outlook, the dethroned bishops found themselves in full agreement. They all set out to seek royal approval, financing, an expeditionary army, endorsement of Pope Pius IX, and a Catholic candidate for their throne. All of this they found.

On the other side of the Atlantic, there sat Napoleon III, with his delusions of grandeur, the Belgian King Leopold of the House of Coburg and the Emperor Franz Joseph of Austria, with a couple of unemployed brothers, each with an ambitious wife who yearned to be an empress. Some members of the House of Hapsburg let their daydreams spin so fancifully that they pictured their family controlling a vast empire comprising both continents of the New World, with one capital in Brazil ruled by Emperor Pedro II and the other under Maximilian in Mexico. Meanwhile, Prince Richard Metternich, the Austrian archconniver, kept the pot boiling as he flitted around the capitals of Europe, fomenting conspiracy against the peoples on the American continents.

A devout man to carry out these plans was found in Archduke Maximilian. At first reluctant and discouraged by his brother, Maximilian was spurred on by Pius IX and Napoleon III, as well as by the imperial ambitions of his beautiful wife. Aspiring to rule over millions of Catholics, he sought the support of the Pope:

> Most Holy Father,
>
> I find myself at a point of very great, and perhaps critical importance in my life, and I cannot hope to arrive at any final decision until I have besought Your Holiness' illuminating advice.
>
> Accordingly I am sending to Rome my secretary, Herr Schertzenlechner, who has on various occasions in the past represented me at Your Holiness' Court, so that he may make known to Your Holiness the problem which confronts me. . . . Should my own views on this matter commend themselves to Your Holiness, then I shall feel assured of the active cooperation of the Holy See, and I venture to hope that I shall receive the sacred blessing—which is so absolutely essential to me. Should Your Holiness condescend to commit your thoughts to writing, then I should not fail to consider it a fresh proof of the great goodness and favour which has hitherto been so unreservedly extended to me by Your Holiness.
>
> The Archduchess has charged me to express to Your Holiness her most humble submission, and she begs to be remembered in your prayers.
>
> We entreat you, Most Holy Father, to accept this humble assurance of our most profound veneration and respect.[10]

## Conspiracy South of the Border

Anxious to reclaim the wealth and power of the Church, the Pope replied:

> We have received through the medium of your secretary, the letter which Your Imperial and Royal Highness has addressed to us, and we gladly send you our reply.
>
> The picture of the country which the Signor Secretary has drawn is truly one which calls forth our pity, and yours is a worthy task when you call upon Religion and Society to busy themselves with speedy remedies.
>
> We hasten to assure you that in that unhappy land all Christian souls, and they are many, eagerly look forward to the time when peace shall again be restored, and such a peace as will enable the Church of Jesus Christ and the Nation of the Mexicans to prosper. . . .
>
> We trust, therefore, that the Lord will favour your undertaking with His blessing, and we earnestly bid you and your illustrious Archduchess to be of good heart.[11]

Sitting on his ecclesiastical throne in Rome, Pope Pius IX actively participated in the plot to establish a monarchy on American soil. "If it should be possible to re-establish a monarchical system in Mexico, the cause of religion and of order in that country would be immensely strengthened."[12]

Although the Papal Secretary of State, Cardinal Antonelli, insisted that the invasion of Mexico give the semblance of a response to the despairing appeal of the Mexican people for intervention to re-establish law and order, the Vatican itself was unwilling to risk an actual referendum of the people. Antonelli told the Austrian ambassador, Baron Bach, that the Pope was worried "concerning the danger contained in the idea of having recourse to a vote of the population to sanction the accession of the future monarch." [13]

The Pope was no mere bystander in the game. His was always the deciding voice. As plans for the rape of Mexico progressed, Maximilian wrote that they were "entirely subject to the approval of Your Holiness." [14] And His Holiness stopped neither at duplicity, at lawlessness, nor at armed intervention to force the medieval and autocratic views of the Holy See upon a helpless people.

The role of the Pope and the spiritual leadership that the Vatican offered were recognized by Maximilian. In a letter to the Pope, he wrote:

> If the efforts of the monarchical party succeed I shall owe it in great part to the goodness, encouragement and cooperation of Your Holiness, and before we leave to take up the post destined me by the Divine Will the Archduchess and myself will not fail to come to Rome, and to place at your Holiness' feet our filial veneration and our infinite gratitude.[15]

While Abraham Lincoln was using every tactic and device to sustain the frail fledgling growth of democracy, the Pope was giving his full blessing, approval, and endorsement to the crushing of a democratic nation that lay, at that moment, on the "soft underbelly" of the United States. The Pope thus could answer the Archduke:

> Your Imperial Highness will conceive with what pleasure I shall embrace you here in Rome, and pronounce upon you and upon your august Archduchess my full blessing, comforting you both before you betake yourselves to that task to which it seems that God has ordained you.[16]

## Conspiracy South of the Border

The ambitions of their Imperial Catholic Apostolic Majesties and of Pope Pius IX did not stop at the Mexican border. There is good historical evidence to indicate that the combined forces of the Roman Church and the authoritarian states in Europe dreamed of taking over the entire Western Hemisphere, *including the United States*.

The royal houses already had one of their relatives on the throne of Brazil. Now they were going to foist a Hapsburg, Maximilian, on Mexico. They strongly hoped that the Confederacy would win the Civil War in America.

After the initial victories of Robert E. Lee, especially at the Battle of Bull Run, European royalty and Vatican authorities were confident of a Southern victory. They considered the Union in a "state of dissolution." The United States could easily be overrun, they calculated, and they envisaged a Catholic empire that would spread North from Central and South America through the remnants of the United States right up to the French Catholics in Canada.

According to one report that found its way into the *New York Times*, influential Southerners asked "young Captain Bonaparte of Baltimore (a close relative of Emperor Napoleon III) to accept the position of Military Dictator of the Southern Confederacy with a crown at his disposal." [19]

Sitting on one of the oppressing and imperialist thrones of Europe was the father-in-law of Maximilian, King Leopold of Belgium, who encouraged the fledgling emperor:

> Once you are firmly established in Mexico, it is probable that a great part of America will place itself under your rule.[20]

The King of Belgium hoped that his son-in-law would become the head "of a great neutral state, closely allied with neutral Belgium. To bring peace, justice and concord to this poor America would be an act, not of ambition, but of simple charity."[21]

Thus three major European monarchies in which the influence of Rome was strong—France, Austria, and Belgium—had shown, by statement and by act, that their sympathies lay with the Confederacy. Through a Southern victory, they hoped to take over and Catholicize the disunited United States.

During 1861 and 1862, these monarchs, in alliance with their fellow-monarch on the throne in Rome, flirted constantly with the formal recognition of the South. The Pope was repeatedly rumored to have actually recognized the Davis government.

However, the legal government of the United States maintained ministers to the Papal States throughout much of the pontificate of Pius IX. A perusal of their reports to the State Department in Washington shows the suspicion and fear that Pius IX might recognize the Confederacy.

On July 19, 1864, Secretary of State, William H. Seward, wrote to the United States Minister at Rome:

> Sir: This Department has been informed by a gentleman of high standing in Canada, that there is a person in Montreal who has in his possession a recognition of the so-called

Southern Confederacy by the Pope, written on parchment. Though this statement is incredible in itself, and improbable from circumstances attending it, it is still deemed worthy of a categorical inquiry of Cardinal Antonelli. This you will consequently make, but in a way not to allow an impression that the statement is believed. If, however, contrary to any reasonable expectation the statement should be confirmed by the Cardinal's answer, you will express the regret of this Government at this proceeding, which must compel a suspension at least of diplomatic intercourse between the two Governments. To this end you will request your passport and will retire to Switzerland or such other quarter as you may think proper, and will there await further instructions of the Department.[22]

The American Minister to Rome, Rufus King, replied that Cardinal Antonelli denied the charge. The Cardinal admitted that Pius IX had written to Jefferson Davis, but stated that the correspondence had been initiated by the Confederate leader.

A short time later, November 26, 1864, King notified Seward that Jefferson Davis had again written to the Pope, "thanking the Holy Father for his letter of last year; expressing the satisfaction which that letter had given to the Southern people and remarking upon the fact that *the Pope was the only potentate in Europe who had uttered a word of sympathy for the Confederates*, in the day of their distress." [23]

The fact that Pope Pius IX was so fully involved in this imperial scheme is very clearly evident, not only from his "fatherly" counselling as the Mexican conspiracy was formed, but also from his angry outburst when the plan began to backfire.

## THE BACKGROUND

Maximilian was a devout son of the Church, but he was also a politician and at heart a humanitarian. When the French forces placed him on the ground in Mexico City in June, 1863, he realized that he could not turn back the moving finger of Mexican history, annul the Law of Reform of 1857, or restore half of the Mexican nation to the priests and the bishops who had expropriated it from the people and then lost it in the struggle led by Juarez.

The Hierarchy screamed "foul" and protested mightily that they had been betrayed by their own protegé. Pope Pius IX wrote an indignant letter of disappointment to Maximilian, on October 18, 1864:

> Sir: When in the month of April last, before assuming the reins of the new empire of Mexico, your Majesty arrived in this capital in order to worship at the tombs of the Holy Apostles and to receive our apostolic benediction, we informed you of the deep sorrow which filled our soul by reason of the lamentable state into which the social disorders during these last years have reduced all that concerns religion in the Mexican nation.
>
> Before that time, and more than once, we had made known our complaints in public and solemn acts, protesting against the iniquitous law called the Law of Reform, which attacked the most inviolable rights of the Church and outraged the authority of its pastors; against the seizure of the ecclesiastical property and the dissipation of the sacred patrimony; against the unjust suppression of the religious orders; against the false maxims that attack the sanctity of the Catholic religion, and, in fine, against many other transgressions committed not only to the prejudice of sacred persons but also of the pastoral priesthood and discipline of the Church. . . .

## Conspiracy South of the Border

The Mexican nation also learned with indescribable pleasure of your Majesty's accession to the throne—called to it by the unanimous desire of a people who, up to that time, had been constrained to groan beneath the yoke of an anarchical Government, and to lament over the ruins and disasters of the Catholic religion, their chief pride at all times and the foundation of their prosperity.

Under such happy auspices we have been waiting day by day the acts of the new empire. . . .

Your Majesty will undoubtedly perceive that if the Church continues to be controlled in the exercise of her sacred rights, if the laws which forbid her to acquire and possess property are not repealed, if churches and convents are still destroyed, if the price of the Church property is accepted at the hands of its unlawful purchasers, if the sacred buildings are appropriated to other uses, if the religious orders are not allowed to reassume their distinctive garments, and to live in community, if the nuns are obliged to beg for their food, and forced to occupy miserable and insufficient edifices, if the newspapers are permitted to insult pastors with impunity, and to assail the doctrines of the Catholic Church; if this state of things is to continue, then the same evils will certainly continue to follow, and perhaps the scandal to the faithful and the wrongs to religion will become greater than ever before. . . .

Your Majesty is well aware that, in order effectively to repair the evils occasioned by the revolution, and to bring back as soon as possible happy days for the Church, the Catholic religion must, above all things, continue to be the glory and the mainstay of the Mexican nation, *to the exclusion of every other dissenting worship*; that the bishops must be perfectly free in the exercise of their pastoral ministry: that the religious orders should be re-established or re-organized, conformably with the instructions and powers which we have given; that the patrimony of the Church and the rights which attach to it may be maintained and protected; that no person may obtain the faculty of teaching and publishing false and subversive tenets; *that instruction, whether public or private, should be directed and watched over by the ecclesiastical authority;* and that, in short, the chains may be broken which up to the present time have held the Church in a state of dependence and subject to the arbitrary rule of the civil government. If the religious edifice should be re-established on such bases—and we will not doubt that such will be the case—your Majesty will satisfy one of the greatest requirements and one of the most lively aspirations of a people so religious as that of Mexico; your Majesty will calm our anxieties and those of the illustrious episcopacy of that country; you will open the way to the education of a learned and zealous clergy, as well as to the moral reform of your subjects; and, besides, you will give a striking example to the other governments in the republics of America in which similar very lamentable vicissitudes have tried the Church; and, lastly, you will labor effectually to consolidate your own throne, to the glory and prosperity of your imperial family.[17]

Thus, at a moment when Abraham Lincoln was battling for freedom and continued liberty North of the Mexican border, the Pope could still implore the head of the neighboring state that "the Catholic religion must, above all things, continue to be the glory and mainstay of the Mexican nation, to the exclusion of every other dissenting worship."

At a moment when, according to some American Catholic historians, the Church was emerging from the dark period known as the "Age of Faith," the Pope could still demand that public instruction be "watched over by the ecclesiastical authority."

## Conspiracy South of the Border

It is difficult to understand how Archbishop Hughes of New York could reconcile his boasted loyalty to Lincoln and the cause of the North with his oath of allegiance to the Pope who was condemning the very principles that Lincoln was fighting for.

Like the rest of America, the Catholic communities were torn asunder by divided loyalties: North against South, brother against brother. In 1862, there were forty-six dioceses, four apostolic vicariates (territories not yet developed sufficiently to have a bishop), all with three to four million Catholics, some in the Union, some in the Confederacy.[18]

American soldiers whether in Blue or in Gray no doubt felt that they were fighting for freedom, including freedom of worship. At the same time however the Catholics were paying homage to their spiritual ruler who was actively involved in a war to destroy that freedom in the land of their southern neighbors.

Back in Italy, where the people were struggling for national unity and independence, the Jesuits were emerging as the objects of deep popular hatred. The Italian people looked upon the Jesuits as connivers against the freedom of Italy from Papal rule. The hand of the Jesuits in the scheming against Lincoln's cause, as well as against that of the Italian people, was becoming increasingly apparent to many leaders.

On June 26, 1865—when the body of Lincoln had but recently turned cold in the grave to which he had been sent by an assassin—Rufus King reported to Seward that negotiations between Pius and Victor Emmanuel were being torpedoed and were making "slow progress—purposely slow, I fancy. The Jesuits are all opposed to it —as they are and were, with few exceptions, to the cause of the (American) Union." [24]

The Jesuits have always been known to all other priests as the most treacherous, single-minded and supranational of all Roman Catholic orders. This is the basic reason why, in country after country, their treachery, ambition and systematic consuming greed have resulted in their suppression and expulsion from every country of Europe, except Czarist Russia, and all the Catholic-dominated countries of America. From the days of Henry VIII and Elizabeth I, the English ferretted them out and hanged them. The Jesuits, Fr. Garnett, Fr. Gerard and Fr. Greenway, were involved even in the Gunpowder Plot of 1605 which was planned to blow up Parliament and destroy British royalty.

Even their own Catholic countries finally became surfeited with Jesuit political intrigue and financial avarice and, in self-preservation, were forced to expel them. Portugal, Angola, Goa and Brazil took the lead in 1759. France followed in 1764. Several Italian states such as Parma, Sicily and Naples followed suit. By sealed imperial orders sent to her colonies around the world, Spain threw out all Jesuits in 1767. This decree suppressed them in the Philippines, Argentina, New Granada (Colombia), Peru, Chile, Ecuador, Guatemala, Cuba, Puerto Rico, Mexico, New Mexico and Arizona. Austria did the same in 1773.

Finally, Pope Clement XIV in 1773 issued the document "Dominus ac Redemptor" abolishing the Jesuit Order altogether, listed eleven popes as having tried to curb their excesses. Among them were Benedict XIV,

Innocent XI, Innocent XIII and Clement XIII. He cited the Jesuits for opposition to "other religious orders," for "revolts and intestine troubles in some of the Catholic states" and "persecutions against the church in Europe and Asia." "There remained no other remedy to so great evils . . . and this step was necessary in order to prevent the Christians from rising one against the other and from massacring each other in the very bosom of our common mother, the holy church." Therefore, he wrote, "after a mature deliberation, we do out of our certain knowledge and the fullness of our apostolic power, suppress and abolish the said Company." [25]

Could the antipathy of the Jesuit leaders in Rome have been reflected in Washington in the Jesuit Georgetown College (now Georgetown University)? Could this explain the fact that the bulk of Georgetown's alumni joined the armies of the South?

Could this illuminate the fact that several of Georgetown's students were involved in the actual conspiracy to kill Abraham Lincoln? That a priest was the confessor of Mary Surratt, who was hanged for her complicity in the assassination? That Jesuits and their students from Georgetown were constantly in the courtroom during the trial of John Surratt? That Surratt himself, just before his death and after his participation in the conspiracy was well recognized, was a teacher of American children in a parochial school?

But for the cautious reserve of the British government, whose sympathy for the Confederacy was well-known, the Papal States would undoubtedly have proceeded with recognition of the Southern rebels. The British, however, remembered with some humiliation the tail-twisting that the Amercan colonies had given the Lion less than a century before, and the threatened Union naval blockade warned them that such a humiliation might be repeated.

But the monarchies were not so cautious. The ambitious and devoutly Catholic consort of Napoleon III, Empress Eugenie, despised democracy in general and the United States in particular. Abraham Lincoln was to her the personification of all that she hated. She entertained the Tuileries ladies and courtesans: "Why is the French-American scientist Dr. Chaillu searching Africa for the missing link, when a specimen was brought from the American backwoods to Washington?" [26]

Eugenie schemed constantly and used her powerful influence over Napoleon toward the extension of monarchy and of the power of the Roman Catholic Church —"first in Mexico and later in the remnants of the disintegrating United States." [27]

Arrayed against the European monarchies, the Church, the slaveholders, and particularly the Jesuit order, there were many forces on the side of freedom, not the least of which was Freemasonry.

In every pompous pontifical condemnation of Freemasonry, the Vatican has always damned it on two scores: first, that it is secret, and second, that it has fought the Catholic Church.

The secrecy charge is preposterous when one considers that nothing in human society is more secret than a Vatican consistory or the election of a Pope.

Freemasonry, in fact, has never fought Catholicism. The opposite is true. The Popes have issued encyclicals against Masonic Orders; Canon Law excommunicates its members who become Masons. In many nations, dictatorships like those of Hitler, Franco, and Salazar have teamed up with the Vatican to outlaw Masonry and persecute, imprison, and even execute Masons.

All dictators, political and religious, whether popes or their puppets, must crush Masonry because they cannot exist without crushing freedom and the men who espouse it. Masonry does not fight against Catholicism; it fights for the freedom of mankind. In all Thirty-Two Degrees of the Scottish Rite, there is not a word against the Roman Catholic Church. But there are very many words for freedom.

Benito Juarez was a Freemason, as was Simon Bolivar, the great liberator of Venezuela, Colombia, and Ecuador. Also among the Freemasons were Sucre, the hero of Bolivia; Mariano Moreno and Manuel Belgrado, who broke the chains of Rome and Spain in Argentina; San Marin, who led the Roman Catholic populace to freedom in Uruguay, Paraguay, and Peru.

The Masonic descendent of the Irish, Bernardo O'Higgins, freed Chile, and the Mason, Jose Marti, led the struggle for the freedom of Cuba. The listing of the Masonic leaders through the years in Central America —Guatemala, El Salvador, Honduras, Nicaragua, and Costa Rica—sounds like a roll call of Blue Lodge officers.

A renegade American citizen, Edward T. Hardy, Confederate agent of the Catholic Austrian Empire, wrote to the Emperor Franz Joseph on September 19, 1863, before the tide had turned irretrievably against the South:

> An Empire having been proclaimed, a war with the United States is inevitable; and next in importance to the pacifi-

cation and reconciliation of the people of Mexico is a recognition of the Southern Confederacy, and an alliance offensive and defensive with it.

The programme of the new Imperial Government might be, 1st The establishment of the Throne beyond peradventure: 2nd The recognition of the Southern States: 3rd If it be necessary, war in conjunction with the South and other allies against the Northern States: 4th If war, then the recovery of the State of California, and, if the Southern States will allow, of the territory of New Mexico; both of which were necessarily ceded to the United States under the treaty of Guadaloupe Hidalgo. . . . Mexico should be an integrity from Oregon to Honduras. . . . I think the South would rather see California in possession of the Empire than of the Northern States. It would be a rich acquisition. It is not improbable that definite and liberal terms offered to the Mormon population, would secure their co-operation. It would be a powerful aid in the rear of California. The Mormons are deeply exasperated against the United States.[28]

The alignment of forces in the early years of the significant decade—the 1860's—is clear. On one side were dictatorship, slavery, secession, monarchy, European imperialism, Jesuit chicanery and a Church-dominated assault upon the Monroe Doctrine, all of which found spiritual leadership in the one person: Pope Pius IX.

On the other side were freedom, emancipation, Freemasonry, democracy, Latin American struggle against foreign domination, all embodied in the one person: Abraham Lincoln.

The alignment was clear; it was leading inexorably to the tragic moment of assassination.

Chapter Five

# The Man and the Demi-God

Pope Pius IX was born Giovanni Mastai-Ferretti in 1792. He ruled as Pope of Rome, Prince of the Apostles, and Successor of St. Peter from 1846 to 1878. Abraham Lincoln was born February 12, 1809 and was murdered April 14, 1865. For fifty-six years the two men were contemporaries.

Personally fearful of the spreading demand for freedom of thought, freedom of speech, freedom of reading, and particularly freedom of religion, Pius IX frantically ground out a flood of encyclicals against these freedoms. He maneuvered concordats with friendly rulers to crush these liberties among the common people. He threw his political weight behind the fronts of the "ancient regime" of favorable emperors and kings who would protect his personal preserve, the Papal States, and further his ecclesiastical ambitions beyond the Alps and around the world.

Abraham Lincoln was the living personification of the growing freedoms that Pius IX hated and feared. If Lincoln won his struggle for government of, by and for the people, Pius knew that the old order was doomed.

## THE BACKGROUND

Throughout the Western Hemisphere, as well as on the doorstep of the Papal See in Europe, the forces of the old way and of the new way, of oppression and of freedom, were lining up for battle.

In the waters of the Atlantic, the United States Navy was threatening to sink any French ships bringing troops to Mexico to support the faltering puppet regime of Maximilian. Shortly after the death of Lincoln, in fact only twenty-six months later, the battle was to be joined. The Emperor was captured by Benito Juarez, court-martialed and shot at Queretaro on June 19, 1867.

In Europe, the papal supporters were faring little better than in the New World. Bismarck had reduced Emperor Franz Joseph to the status of a provincial puppet, and then proceeded to take on Napoleon III in the Franco-Prussian War in 1870, and drove the once-proud scheming emperor into exile.

In the same year the victorious Italian patriots marched on Rome. Victor Emmanuel II took over the Holy City. The petulant, cursing Pope locked St. Peter's doors and proclaimed himself the "prisoner in the Vatican."

Abraham Lincoln and Pope Pius IX—they are indeed a study in contrast. It is difficult to think of two contemporary world figures more completely the opposite in temperament, personality, character, ambition, tactics, self-evaluation, and attitude toward their fellow-men.

For one hundred years the great and little people of all nations and all races have exhausted their languages and their adjectives in paying glowing and almost unanimous homage to Abraham Lincoln as one of the noblest humans who has ever lived. The volume of Lincolniana

## The Man and the Demi-God

in the Library of Congress lists a host of eulogies preached in churches everywhere.

Whatever human failings Lincoln possessed are lost in the richness of his Messianic virtues. He was of and from the poor and never forgot the poor. He defended them without charge, as he did the ex-priest Chiniquy, when he could identify with their cause. His sympathy and kindness went beyond the widows and orphans, and included even soldiers who, in the anguish of battle and in the fear that grips man, had deserted his own side.

Lincoln believed deeply in God, and in the complete tolerance of all religions. He believed also in man's right to believe in no God. He fought for complete freedom for all men from the chains of mental as well as physical slavery. Before the rifles and cannons of the Civil War fell still, his great heart reached out to those who would have destroyed him in an all-encompassing gesture of love and amnesty.

The Lincoln Monument in Washington, D.C. has become to the yearning, struggling, hoping people of all the world, not a showplace, not a museum, but the sacred shrine of the man who, without any ritual of canonization, has become one of the most venerated saints in the history of the human race. The tears that spontaneously well forth in the presence of the heroic, brooding figure of the Emancipator are more infinitely expressive of appreciation, love and respect than flowers, votive candles, speeches, and memorial wreaths.

It is unfortunate for Pius IX and his Church that he lived in the same century as Abraham Lincoln. If it were otherwise, the contrast might not be so shocking.

## THE BACKGROUND

Anyone—ex-priest, poet or peasant—who loves Lincoln and freedom would be accused of bias and prejudice if he attempted to describe Pius. It is better to let others, and his deeds and his own words, build the true image.

The Pope's pathological fear and hatred of freedom for the little people, either in politics or in religion, was evident from his words and behavior in his part in the suppression of the Mexican people through the Maximilian Empire.

In 1863, while our Civil War was in progress, Colombia established religious liberty and perforce restricted the exclusive "rights" of the Roman Catholic hierarchy regarding finances, control of worship, and of education. Pius IX, on September 17, 1863 in his encyclical, *Incredibili Afflictamur,* flailed and ranted with the mentality of an early medieval Pope who thought the constitutions and laws of all countries were subject to his whims.

In listing the "nefarious and most iniquitous" laws of Colombia (he still called it New Granada) he specifically listed: "It (the Colombian Government) sanctions the worship of non-Catholic sects." The Pope praises, as "good soldiers of Christ," the priests who had refused to swear allegiance to the Government and strongly condemned priests who had conformed.

Finally, with his infallible authority, he simply wiped the laws of the sovereign state of Colombia off the books and out of the consciences of Catholic citizens:

> In this letter we raise our Apostolic Voice and sorrowfully protest and energetically condemn all these most serious assaults and injuries inflicted by the Government on the

## The Man and the Demi-God

>Church, on its properties, on its consecrated persons and on this Holy See. . . . We with Apostolic Authority denounce and condemn all such laws and decrees with all their consequences, and by the same authority *we abrogate those laws and declare them entirely null and without binding power.*[1]

The date was September 17, 1863. Abraham Lincoln was the President in Washington, fighting a Civil War that "freedom might long endure." If Pope Pius could abolish the Constitution of Colombia, why could he not abolish the Constitution of the United States? In fact, he tried just that the next year when in the Syllabus of Errors (Error #55) he "abolished" separation of Church and State.

In that same year, 1863, on April 23, three Protestant Spaniards, Matamoras, Trigo and Alhama, had been convicted of attending Protestant meetings. Matamoras was sentenced to nine years punishment, Alhama to nine years, and Trigo to seven years—all *in the galleys!*[2]

But Pius IX's hatred of human freedom, both intellectual and religious, is most violently stamped on history in his battle against his own "paisanos," his own countrymen, the Italian people. Count Charles Arribavene attributes the endorsing "judgment of nine-tenths of Italians" to Garibaldi when that general said in Naples:

>But, before fighting against this external enemy, you have internal enemies to beat down; and I will tell you that the chief of them is the Pope. If I have acquired any merit with you, it is that of telling you the truth frankly and without a veil. In using this privilege, "I tell you that your chief enemy is the Pope."

## THE BACKGROUND

> I am a Christian as you are; yes, I am of that religion which has broken the bonds of slavery, and has proclaimed the freedom of men. The Pope, who oppresses his subjects, and is an enemy of Italian independence, is no Christian; he denies the very principle of Christianity; he is Antichrist.[3]

The people of the province of Rome endorsed these sentiments against Pius in a plebiscite when they voted 133,681 to 1,507 for the freedom of Italy.[4]

The Pope's refusal to recognize the political aspirations of the Roman people emphasized the unbridgeable void between his thinking and that of Abraham Lincoln. His contention that the desired constitutional government for the people of the Papal States "would violate the divine law" proved that in theory as well as in practical politics he still clung to the "divine right of Kings."[5]

Pius IX did more than fulminate against the people who merely wanted the rights that Lincoln endorsed as self-evident. He executed hundreds of patriots. He jammed 8,000 of them into the Papal jails in which "many were chained to the wall and not released even for exercise or sanitary purposes."[6]

The English ambassador called the dungeons of Pius IX "the opprobrium of Europe."[7] Another contemporaneous writer describes the Roman people's reaction to the rule of Pius when they achieved their freedom:

> The Romans inaugurated their republic with religious observances, for they were anxious to show that they adhered to the Christian faith, and that liberty did not mean atheism. Among the first measures of the new government was the abolition of the Holy Office of the Inquisition.

## The Man and the Demi-God

> The populace would have levelled it with the ground, but the ministers decided to put the building to some charitable purpose; before making any alteration in it, they thought it well to leave it open for a few days, to let the citizens see with their own eyes the secret mechanism of the papal system. They did not need any evidence to know that the only crime of serious moment in the States of the Church was liberal thought in religion and politics. That their friends and relations had been spirited away, and immured in prison, they also knew too well. And when the prison doors were open these emaciated heretics had a sad tale to tell of cruel suffering and ingenious torture.[8]

Of the paternal rule of the Vicar of Christ, Arribavene wrote:

> Side by side with this class of free mendicants was a less fortunate one—that of the prisoners. From dawn till nightfall, the miserable captives would cling to the iron bars of their horrible dwellings, and perpetually call upon the passer-by for alms in the name of God. A Papal prison! how I shudder in writing the words. In those prisons, human beings were heaped confusedly together, covered with rags, and swarming with vermin. Some disgusting soup, a piece of scarcely digestible meat, and a bajocco in money—a coin worth only a fraction above a half-penny English—was all that the Government allowed per day to each prisoner.[9]

There is little wonder that the anti-clerical Italians (and this means most Italians) hit back with the strongest weapon they knew—ridicule:

> Thy will be done in barracks as on the field of battle. Give us ammunition each day. And do not lead us into the temptation of counting the numbers of the enemy. But deliver us 'from the Austrians and the priests.' [10]

## THE BACKGROUND

By the almost unanimous votes of their plebiscites, the Italian Catholic people endorsed the stinging eloquence of their great patriot, Giuseppe Mazzini, when he thundered against the Papacy:

> The Gospel whispers universal love and brotherhood, but you have sown discord, you have inspired hatred, you have stirred up warfare among the sons of the same land; you have gradually erected your fortress of usurped power upon the corpses of passing generations; you have imported the foreign invader; you have pitted princes against princes, families against families, peoples against peoples. You have stooped to unite in political fornication with the civil government of any and all despotic countries; you have prostituted the cross, the symbol of sacrifice and salvation into the symbol of tyranny and ruin. . . . You who should have protected the weak against the oppressor, you who should have encouraged peace among citizens, you have summoned the paid assassins (the French and Austrians) to whet their murderous daggers upon the very stone of the altar, while you have warned your citizen slaves "do not dare to arise." . . . Those who call themselves the Vicars of God on earth have become the Vicars of the genius of evil.[11]

It is almost impossible to reconcile the pious encyclicals and the decree of papal infallibility with the man who encouraged and permitted this savage medieval system, but it certainly explains the traditional anti-clericalism of the Italian people. It is explained, for example, by this passage from Arribavene:

> Judges were either corrupt or powerless to check the influence of priests and Monsignori, their decisions being generally fettered by the Supreme Tribunal, the Roman 'Ruota', so that even common cases were rarely decided

before the lapse of many years. And over all this rotten system hung the mysterious and secret power of the Tribunal of the Holy Inquisition, whose influence was felt not only in religious questions, but in every other, as that of the Council of Ten had been felt in the Republic of Venice. Under such a system, the man who had murdered or plundered another had nothing to fear from Papal justice if he were untarnished by liberal opinions, and were a firm adherent of the temporal power.[12]

Execution was not at all uncommon in the Holy See:

> The pain of death for offences against religion was part of the penal code; to the Church was still permitted the relic of medieval lawlessness—the right of asylum for criminals; to the parish priest were left all civil registers; to the Jesuits the right to penetrate everywhere—to rule the royal household, the private homes of citizens, the public institutions, the schools, etc.; so that the country was absolutely subject to the priestly power.[13]

The depravity of this papal barbarism should be even more shocking to an American, especially an American Catholic, when it is remembered that these horrible atrocities were perpetrated by a Pope, not back in the Dark Ages, but in the day of Abraham Lincoln—almost one hundred years *after* our Declaration of Independence.

But the Papal, French and Austrian armies could not crush the ground-swell of Italian freedom and unity. As Victor Emmanuel and his army approached St. Peter's, Pius IX fell back on his spiritual artillery—excommunication. These are the words of the Encyclical "Respicientes," November 1, 1870:

> Since our advice, pleadings and protests have been entirely useless, therefore with the authority of Almighty God, of

the holy apostles Peter and Paul, and of our own, we declare to you, Venerable Brothers (the bishops of the Church), and through you to the entire Church, that all those, even though they be honored with a dignity especially worthy of mention, who have perpetrated the invasion, usurpation and occupation of the provinces of Our domain, or of this dear City (Rome), and their commanders, supporters, collaborators, advisors, followers and all the rest who have led or carried out under any pretext or in any manner the execution of the aforementioned deeds, have incurred major excommunication and all the rest of the censures and ecclesiastical penalties, covered by the sacred canons, apostolic constitutions and decrees of all the general Councils especially the Council of Trent.[14]

Judging the number of "supporters, collaborators, advisors and followers" by the previous plebiscites, Pope Pius IX in this "paternal admonition" threw out of the Roman Catholic Church ninety-eight per cent of the Italian people.

When the excommunication of the nation failed to stop the armies, Pius IX vented his anger in the almost unbelievable curse on the advancing king, Victor Emmanuel:

May he (King Victor Emmanuel) be damned wherever he may be; whether in the house or in the field, whether in the highway or in the byway, whether in the wood or in the water, or whether in the church. May he be cursed in living and dying, in eating and drinking, in fasting and thirsting, in slumbering and sleeping, in watching or walking, in standing or sitting, in lying down or walking *mingendo cancando*, and in all bloodletting. May he be cursed in all the faculties of his body. May he be cursed inwardly and outwardly. May he be cursed in his hair. May he be cursed in his brain. May he be cursed in the crown of his head and in his

## The Man and the Demi-God

temples. In his forehead and in his ears. In his eyebrows and in his cheeks. In his jawbones and his nostrils. In his foreteeth and in his grinders. In his lips and in his throat. In his shoulders and in his wrists. In his arms, his hands, and his fingers. May he be damned in his mouth, in his breast, in his heart, and in all the viscera of his body. May he be damned in his veins and in his groin; in his thighs; in his hips and in his knees; in his legs, feet and toe nails.

May he be cursed in all the joints and articulations of his body. From the top of his head to the sole of his foot may there be no soundness in him. May the Son of the living God, with all the glory of His Majesty, curse him; and may heaven, with all the powers that move therein, rise up against him, curse him and damn him! Amen! So let it be! Amen.[15]

If these words of the Holy Father, Pope Pius IX, were shocking to his "children," the Italians, who had been brought up in a tradition of religious intolerance and political despotism, they should have been completely baffling and incomprehensible to Americans who had breathed nothing but the free air of complete religious, mental, and political liberty, and who were accustomed to the Christian charity expressed in the words of Abraham Lincoln: "With malice towards none, with charity for all...."

The complete antithesis and irreconcilable intellectual and moral conflict between these two world leaders of their age can be most clearly presented by the juxtaposition of their own words, given in greater detail in the appendix to this book.

PRESIDENT LINCOLN'S FUNERAL—PROCESSION IN CHICAGO, ILLINOIS
[Photographed by Atschulet, Chicago.]

PART TWO

The Crime

Chapter Six

# A Man Is Shot

Predictions that Abraham Lincoln would be assassinated were made before he was first inaugurated. The "Baltimore Plot" of 1861 was led by an Italian immigrant, Cipriano Fernandino. Lincoln was saved by Pinkerton detectives who smuggled him into Washington.

At the time of Lincoln's second inauguration in March of 1865, the final conspiracy to kidnap or kill the President had firmly jelled. Stake-outs by the gang were held at the Ford Theatre during the Second Inaugural Address and a few weeks later near the Old Soldiers' Home on the outskirts of Washington.

The actual murder of Lincoln was not, as some have claimed, the sudden impulse of a drunken actor. His death had been determined long before. Only the time and place had not been definitely fixed.

Many meetings had been held. Mary Surratt had smuggled a rifle and whiskey out to the tavern at Surrattsville across the Potomac, a boat had been purchased, and horses had been obtained. At the moment Lincoln was to be shot by Booth, the Vice-President Andrew Johnson was to be

## THE CRIME

killed by another member of the gang, Secretary of State Seward by another, and the victorious Union General Ulysses S. Grant by another. Others were to give the signals, hold the horses, clear communications and help all the assassins into friendly Southern territory.

The final eventful day was April 14, 1865—Good Friday. Mr. Lincoln had decided to attend the popular play, *Our American Cousin,* at the Ford Theatre. At 10:10 P.M., the time all the murders were to be perpetrated, John Wilkes Booth slipped into the President's box above the stage, aimed his small derringer at the back of Lincoln's head, and fired. Lincoln's friend, Major Rathbone, heard the shot and sprang at Booth. The assassin stabbed him but lost his balance as he jumped over the railing of the box. As he hit the stage his leg broke. Lincoln dropped unconscious and died the next morning in a building across the street.

In the confusion, Booth slipped out the stage door where Edward Spangler was waiting with his horse. He was able to mount, in spite of his injury and, accompanied by David Herold, another accomplice, followed the prearranged plan out of the city.

Their tortured and tortuous escape by boat and backwoods roads led to the gun and whiskey at Surrattsville, to treatment for his broken leg by his friend and co-conspirator, Dr. Samuel Mudd, and finally death when surrounded by Union troops at Richard Garrett's barn in Virginia.

None of the other scheduled murders took place. William H. Seward was stabbed by Lewis Paine and

## A Man Is Shot

would have been killed but for the intervention of relatives and servants.

Vice-President Johnson was saved because George Atzerodt got drunk and lost his nerve.

General Ulysses Grant had fortunately left town.

THE ASSASSIN'S TOAST

Chapter Seven

# The Hired Hands: A Motley Crew

*I believe he is protected by the Clergy and that the murder is the result of a deep laid plot not only against the life of President Lincoln, but against the existence of the Republic, as we are aware that priesthood and Royalty are and always have been opposed to liberty. That such men as Surratt, Booth, Wiechman and others should of their own accord plan and execute the infernal plot which resulted in the death of President Lincoln is impossible. There are others behind the curtain who have pulled the strings to make these scoundrels act...*

Affidavit of Henri B. de Ste. Marie, given to Rufus King, U.S. Minister at Rome, July 14, 1866, and transmitted to William Seward, Secretary of State of the United States.

That John Wilkes Booth fired the shot that killed Abraham Lincoln is one of the few undisputed facts in the controversy that swirls about the assassination of the President. That Booth had colleagues and conspirators is also generally acknowledged. But no one can with certainty state today exactly how far and in what directions the nerve commands of intrigue reached, into what areas

FLIGHT OF THE ASSASSINS

## The Hired Hands

of America or the world, into what seats of power and institutions.

The indictments by the United States Government included the immediate conspirators and many leaders and agents of the Confederacy. They also included "others unknown."

Behind these "others unknown," historians and scholars delving into the archives of the Civil War have found many varied characters. Lincoln's Secretary of War, Edwin Stanton, has been accused of being a violently vindictive man, opposed to Lincoln's policy of amnesty, who (it is contended) might well have hired friends of the Confederacy to do away with Lincoln so that the leaders of that Confederacy, Davis and his cronies, might be dealt with justly and harshly.

There are others who point the accusing finger at the Vice-President, Andrew Johnson, claiming that he had delusions of grandeur, and that he knew that he could reach the coveted Presidency only through the death of Lincoln.

Others make accusations of a more generalized nature against "big business," which was hardly big as judged from the vantage point of our day, but to whose bigness Lincoln was indeed opposed.

Finally, Davis and the Confederate leaders were naturally suspect. The kidnapping or death of the Emancipator loomed as the last frantic chance of survival of the secessionists.

Through the years a few voices have been heard, some of them denounced, more often ignored—voices of people who saw in the conspiracy and the assassination the

## THE CRIME

hand of Papal intrigue and shadowy Jesuitical treachery of the Roman Catholic Church, who joined with the other Lincoln haters and were at the least co-conspirators in his liquidation, accessories probably before the fact, and certainly after the fact.

The motive of the ecclesiastical organization was the strongest and the most obvious of all—the necessary elimination of the then world's greatest threat to Rome's political despotism and mental authoritarianism—the growing political liberalism personified by Abraham Lincoln.

That the Church, as its historians have done, should blame others for America's tragedy was true to its normal pattern. It constantly blames the Inquisition on Spain, the murder of Savanorola on the Florentine rabble, the burning of St. Joan of Arc on the British, the rape of Mexico on the "bandits" of Juarez, and its own long-needed suppression of the Jesuits on the Freemasons.

John Wilkes Booth and his companions comprised as motley a gang as ever pirated a ship, held up a mail train, or waylaid a gentleman in an alley. They also behaved in typical conspiratorial fashion. They had passwords, rendezvous and secret meetings, not only in Mary Surratt's notorious home, but also in taverns, barns, hotels, and even at Mass in Catholic churches.

The group smuggled guns and flitted in and out of Washington, Maryland, Virginia and New York, down into the Confederate lines and up into Canada, with a speed and frequency almost unbelievable in those days of comparatively primitive transportation.

### The Hired Hands

Some anti-clerical writers have accused all of the colleagues in intrigue who joined Booth of being Roman Catholic, just as they accuse the Vatican of complicity in all of our Presidential assassinations. The facts do not justify such a sweeping indictment.

However, the presence of non-Catholics among the immediate conspirators does not of itself absolve the Church. Even the Mafia has been known to hire non-members to perform its executions. And the murder of Lincoln was certainly a mercenary job. Too much money flowed too freely, like the whiskey of Booth and Atzerodt, for it to have been entirely a labor of love.

On the other hand, there was a preponderance of Catholics and Catholic-educated conspirators among these gangsters, especially their leaders, and they had more than normal affinity for priests, especially Jesuit priests.

It may be helpful to point out what is known of the religious as well as the general background of Booth and his friends.

JOHN WILKES BOOTH: Booth came from a family of actors. Politically they were split in their loyalties to the North and the South. They seem also to have been split denominationally. The family background was Episcopalian. Several writers, who have not copied from each other because they relate totally different incidents, indicate that John Wilkes Booth was converted to the Roman Catholic faith.

He is said to have been wearing a Catholic medal on a chain around his neck when he died.

## THE CRIME

Rear Admiral George W. Baird, USN, Retired, 33° Mason, who identified the body of Booth on the gunboat, the Montauk, wrote on November 29, 1921:

> I was called on board the Montauk by Lt. W. W. Crowninshield to identify the body of John Wilkes Booth, which I did. I noticed a piece of cord about the size of a cod line on his (Booth's) neck and invited Crowninshield's attention to it, who pulled it out and on it was a small Roman Catholic medal. Surgeon General Barnes arrived at that moment and probed the wound in Booth's neck.[1]

This evidence seemed so important that I wrote to the Supreme Council of the Scottish Rite to verify the existence and Masonic membership of George W. Baird. The Grand Secretary General of the Supreme Council answered on June 13, 1962:

> Referring to the matter of Rear Admiral George Washington Baird, USN, Retired, will say that we have checked our records and find that a man by the name of George Washington Baird, was at the time of initiation a Chief Engineer in the United States Navy. He was born April 22, 1843, in Washington, D.C., and joined the Bodies here in 1889. At the time of his death he was a 33° Inspector General Honorary. I'm sure this is the same man that you refer to.

Twice Booth is mentioned as having attended Mass. Once was when he met Dr. Samuel Mudd, a fellow-conspirator, at St. Mary's Church near Bryantown, Maryland in November, 1864.[2]

In a letter written to a friend named Clinton very shortly before he shot Lincoln, he shows an insight into

## The Hired Hands

the duplicity of the Roman Hierarchy that non-Catholics rarely possess:

> That is one side of the picture, now what will the South say, for her preachers have at least as good a right, as their Northern brethren, to electrify their audiences, but they will be more guarded. Some of our reverend friends down there are just as pro-slavery as our Northern friends are anti and have rendered just as much good service to the cause. Witness the Archbishop of New Orleans, who in the beginning of the war, in conjunction with the Abbe Perche, consecrated sundry flags and banners. Then there was McGill of Richmond, a splendid preacher by the way, and who, though report says that he was born in Philadelphia, has been exceedingly true to the right side, or as I suppose his enemies and ours would say, a most confounded traitor; one who has forgotten the duties of his mission, and who if he had his just deserts, would be hanged without judge or jury, or at the very least, that a strong representation should be sent to Rome, and he be deprived of his Bishopric, if not degraded from his Episcopal functions. And then too, there was Lynch of South Carolina, a worthy successor of the illustrious England, who, when that prying, meddlesome Phadrig of New York, Hughes, came out in a letter on the Federal side, (you may remember that Bennett of the Herald some years ago said, "that Hughes was an impudent and ignorant prelate, who had better never have left his original vocation of raising cabbages at Emmittsburg,") and Lynch answered him. These are the greater lights, and you know that the purple, the crosier and the title of Right Reverend have a great influence on the mob.
>
> Now let us see what these gentlemen will say. As a matter of course, they will not take these words as their text, "Know ye not, that a great man has fallen this day in Israel," but they will be sure to ransack some other portion of the Bible, to find something that will meet their wishes.[3]

## THE CRIME

The Bishop Lynch of Charleston to whom Booth refers is the same cleric that the American minister to the Vatican, Rufus King, kept an eye on in Rome during the War. He was the South's representative at the Vatican.

Cardinal Antonelli, the millionaire Papal Secretary of State, who left $20,000,000 to his illegitimate daughter,[4] kept Bishop Lynch handily waiting in the Papal anterooms for a quick formal public recognition of the Confederacy should the tide of fortune happily favor the South. Bishop Lynch had been so thoroughly disloyal to the United States that he was afraid to return to America after the War.

The detailed reports of U.S. Minister Rufus King in Rome to William Seward, United States Secretary of State, confirm what otherwise might be considered an apocryphal letter of Booth. On June 26, 1865, King wrote:

> Bishop Lynch is very anxious to get back to Charleston, but very apprehensive that he may be held to account for his "sayings and doings," as an avowed Confederate agent. The "supplies," I suspect, have given out and "the Bishop," who "entertained" a good deal last year, by way of creating a "public opinion" in favor of the South, is now, I understand, a "guest" of the Propaganda (the Vatican) and without "visible means of support."[5]

A very strong indication of Booth's Catholicism is found in his Catholic use of the crucifix and in his reference to the Virgin Mary in the following dramatic description of the oath the night before the assassination, as presented in one of the most complete reports of the period:

> "The oath! the oath! bring out the crucifix, Mrs. Surratt."

## The Hired Hands

"You will pardon me, Mr. Booth, but that must not be in my house."

"And why not, madam?" replied Booth, "we are engaged in a holy cause."

Awed by the tone of command in which these words were spoken, and the fiery glance accompanying them, the sculptured representation of the savior was placed on the table, and Booth lit three candles he had brought with him, and extinguished the gas. The starry flames of the candles, alone prevented utter darkness; and cast a pale gleam on the countenances of the conspirators.

Booth advanced to the table, and seizing the cross, exclaimed in a low, but deep and earnest tone, "I do solemnly swear by the passion of our Lord and Savior Jesus Christ—"

"Mr. Booth, I entreat you, go no further," said Mrs. Surratt.

"Peace, madam," he replied sternly. "The oath shall be taken! Is this child's play, or have we come here merely to have a little sport. The oath shall be taken, and by all in this chamber; no one leaves till he has sworn to obey. Where are your protestations of loyalty to the South, have they all vanished, have they all melted into thin air. I say again that the oath shall be taken. Disobey me at your peril."

Herold and Atzerodt rose from their seats, stood on either side of the mistress of the house, and waited orders from their leader. The affrighted woman glanced at the doors and windows, but could expect no help.

A loud peal at the door bell, somewhat encouraged her, but Booth directed Payne to answer the summons, and all hope was cut off from that quarter. It was merely a man asking if Mrs. Brown lived there, and a reply being given in the negative, the door was closed, and Booth resumed.

"I shall now take the oath, and you, madam, will be silent, if you utter a word or make a movement, you shall die."

Herold and Atzerodt produced loaded pistols, and Booth pronounced these words.

"I do solemnly swear, by the passion of our Lord Jesus Christ, by his agony in the garden, by the sorrow which pierced his soul when Peter denied him, and by the spotless purity of his Holy Mother, that I will aid and abet, by all the means in my power, the plot which has just been planned; and I further swear by all that man holds sacred, both in this world and the next, that should any one attempt to reveal the plot or any part of it, that I will pursue him with the most utmost vengeance, no matter how closely connected with me." He then kissed the crucifix.

Each in turn advanced and took the oath, not excepting Mrs. Surratt, who was livid with terror.

Booth then observed to her, "Madam, should you see fit to inform the authorities of this night's transactions, your life shall pay the forfeit. You may indeed escape us for a time, but the Golden Circle is prompt."

A cold good night was exchanged, and Mrs. Surratt was alone. The threat was not without its significance, she was dumb.

Booth stepping into the nearest hotel, wrote the following brief note.

The plot is all arranged, expect great developments. The blow will be inflicted in twenty-four hours or less time. The die is cast, and I cannot, if I would, retrace my steps.

Booth[6]

MARY E. JENKINS SURRATT: Mary Surratt was the "mother hen" of the immediate conspiratorial gang. She was also the most ardently Catholic. The details of the plot, first to kidnap Lincoln and, when that failed, to kill him, were hatched in her Washington boarding house. Booth, Paine, Herold, Atzerodt, and her son, John H. Surratt, gathered

### The Hired Hands

in her house, held their secret meetings, prayed for God's blessings on their crusade, and stealthily dispersed in the best cloak-and-dagger tradition. Andrew Johnson called her house "the nest where the egg was hatched."

Mary Surratt was no mere innkeeper to the conspiracy, as she later pleaded in defense of her life. She introduced Booth to other plotters, such as Dr. Mudd. She ran errands for the boys, such as her trip with Louis Wiechman to store away the carbine and whiskey for Booth at Lloyd's Tavern in her old home at Surrattsville. It was here that, during the earlier days of the War, her home had been a stopover for spies, Confederate agents, and blockade runners.[7]

Mary Surratt was a very devout, ritualistic Roman Catholic. The aim of the Church's school system had been realized in her. Her Protestant parents had sent her to a Catholic school for a genteel moral education. Instead, as so frequently happens, they got back a fanatical Catholic, one who with a clear conscience would one day plot the murder of a President. The Catholic school was Miss Winifred Martin's School for Young Ladies in Alexandria, Virginia.[8]

In a letter to her parish priest, she bemoaned her inability to educate her eldest son Isaac and told of her longing to attend Mass:

> O I hope Dear Father you will try and get him something to do as it will be so much better for him to be out of sight of his Pa as he is drunk almost every day. . . . O, I could not tell you what a time I see on this earth. I try to keep it all from the world on account of my poor Children. . . . I

hope I shall be able to send John to school next year. . . . I have not had the pleasure of going to Church on Sunday for more than a year.[9]

After her husband, John Surratt, Sr., drank himself to death in July, 1862, Mary Surratt moved to Washington and opened her "Catholic" boarding house. Besides her son John and her daughter Anna, she took in a Catholic boarder, Louis Wiechman, the Irish-American John Holohan and his family, and one Miss Honora Fitzpatrick. During the final days of the conspiracy, some of the other conspirators also boarded with her.

Mrs. Surratt was able to reconcile the plotting of murder with devout Catholicism. On the evening of Good Friday, April 14, 1865, at about the time Booth was scheduled to shoot Lincoln, she sat in her parlor saying the Rosary. She asked Louis Wiechman the typical Catholic request "to pray for her intentions."[10] Two days later, on Easter Sunday, she accompanied the other ladies of her household to Mass at St. Patrick's Church.[11]

The common Catholic self-contradiction of being able to pray and lie in the same breath was strikingly demonstrated in Mary Surratt when she was arrested as a conspirator. The official in charge of the arresting group of soldiers was Captain Henry Warren Smith. In John Surratt's trial he tells of arresting Mrs. Surratt on April 17, 1865:

> Mrs. Surratt said to me, "By your leave, sir, I would like to kneel down and say my prayers, to ask the blessing of God upon me as I do upon all my actions." She knelt down in the parlor and prayed. In the meantime I heard steps coming up the front steps. It was Lewis Payne (sometimes

## The Hired Hands

called Wood) one of the principal conspirators. He had been in Mrs. Surratt's house several times before. "Mrs. Surratt," said I, "do you know this man? Did you hire him to dig a ditch for you?" She raised both her hands and said, "Before God, I do not know this man. I have never seen him. I did not hire him to dig a ditch." [12]

The crowning assurance of her Catholic acceptance was the fact that five priests testified at her trial for murder that she was of sterling Catholic moral character. They were Fr. Francis E. Boyle, Fr. Charles H. Stonestreet, Fr. Peter Lanahan, Fr. W. D. Young and Fr. J. A. Walter.[13] One might wonder if due to her intimacy with the priests, she was merely echoing what she might have heard from them when she remarked to her daughter Anna on the night her house was searched: "Anna, come what will, I am resigned. I think that Booth was only an instrument in the hands of the Almighty to punish this wicked and licentious people." [14]

JOHN HARRISON SURRATT, JR.: With Booth and his mother, John H. Surratt made up the trio who were the core of the Lincoln conspiracy. If there be any doubt that the Catholic Church used Surratt in the President's murder, it is abundantly proven that before and after the event John Surratt used the Catholic Church.

Surratt was the professional of the gang. He had studied for the Catholic priesthood in St. Charles College in Maryland before becoming a message bearer, acknowledged spy, and Confederate agent. By his own words he became so expert in hiding dispatches "in his shoes" and elsewhere that the "stupid set of detectives . . .

**THE CRIME**

employed by the U.S. Government—seemed to have no idea whatever how to search me."

He slipped constantly and elusively from Richmond to New York, to Montreal, armed with secret messages and plenty of money. He also left a string of romances behind him.

He met John Wilkes Booth in January of 1865. They were constantly in contact with each other until the day of the assassination.

Surratt was considered by the U.S. Government to be so deeply involved in Lincoln's death that he was listed right after Booth in the first reward posters. He was also named first, even before Booth and Jefferson Davis, in the "charges and specifications" prepared by the order of the President of the United States by the Judge Advocate General J. Holt.[15]

The relationship between Surratt and the Hierarchy of the Roman Catholic Church becomes more apparent after the assassination in his escape with the help of Catholic priests, his being smuggled across the Atlantic by Catholic priests, his concealment in London by Catholic priests, his disguised presence in the Pope's Zouave Army, his "escape" when discovered by the U.S. Government, and the solicitude of priests, especially Jesuit priests, toward him during his trial.

The John Surratt story is the most suspicious aspect of the whole Lincoln assassination plot and dénouement. It is the Vatican's point of greatest vulnerability.

LEWIS PAINE: The Government's charge against Paine (also Payne) was that "on the same night of the 14th

## The Hired Hands

day of April, A.D. 1865, about the same hour at ten o'clock and fifteen minutes P.M., at the city of Washington, and within the military department and military lines he unlawfully and maliciously made an assault upon the said William H. Seward, Secretary of State, . . . and with a large knife held in his hand, did unlawfully, traitorously and in pursuance of said conspiracy, strike, stab, cut and attempt to kill and murder the said William H. Seward." [16]

Paine also went under the names of Powell, Hull, or Reverend Wood. His father was a Baptist preacher. At times he also claimed to be a preacher. It is certain that he had been a dedicated rebel soldier. There is no evidence that Paine was ever a Roman Catholic.

DAVID E. HEROLD: The charge against David E. Herold was that he "did, on the night of the 14th of April, A.D. 1865 . . . aid, abet and assist the said John Wilkes Booth in the killing and murder of the said Abraham Lincoln, and did, then and there, aid, abet and assist him, the said John Wilkes Booth, in attempting to escape . . ." [17]

Herold was a native Marylander, a Southerner who grew up among Roman Catholics. His family was said to be Episcopalians. He went to school at the Charlotte Hall Academy near Bryantown, in St. Mary's County. It was at St. Mary's Catholic Church near Bryantown that Booth and Dr. Mudd attended Mass together on November 13, 1864.

Herold was Booth's guide on his fatal flight. His familiarity with Catholics and Catholic establishments, such as Surratt's Tavern at Surrattsville and Dr. Samuel Mudd's home where the doctor treated Booth's broken leg, would lead to the conclusion that Herold was undoubtedly under Catholic influence.

GEORGE A. ATZERODT: The U.S. Government charged that "the said George A. Atzerodt did, on the night of the 14th of April, A.D. 1865, and about the same hour of the night aforesaid, within the military department and military lines aforesaid, lie in wait for Andrew Johnson, then Vice-President of the United States aforesaid, with the intent unlawfully and maliciously to kill and murder him, the said Andrew Johnson." [18]

Atzerodt was what the English might call a "churlish lout." He was so coarse in his habits that, in spite of his deep involvement in the conspiracy, Mrs. Surratt threw him out of her boarding house, although she permitted him to attend the meetings of the conspirators. He was said to be a lackadaisical Austrian Catholic and accompanied Louis Wiechman to Mass at St. Patrick's Church in Washington.[19]

He was given the chore of murdering the Vice-President, but he got drunk and missed his cue.

DR. SAMUEL MUDD: Dr. Mudd was much more deeply involved in the assassination conspiracy than his role or his ultimate punishment would indicate. The court specification against him was longer than most:

> And in further prosecution of said conspiracy the said Samuel A. Mudd did at Washington City and within the military department and military lines aforesaid, on or before the 6th day of March, A.D. 1865, and on divers other days and times between that day and the 20th of April, A.D. 1865,

**The Hired Hands**

advise, encourage, receive, entertain, harbor and conceal, aid and assist the said John Wilkes Booth, David E. Herold, Lewis Payne, John H. Surratt, Michael O'Laughlin, George A. Atzerodt, Mary E. Surratt, and Samuel Arnold, and their confederates, with knowledge of the murderous and traitorous conspiracy aforesaid, and with the intent to aid, abet and assist them in the execution thereof and in escaping from justice after the murder of the said Abraham Lincoln, in pursuance of said conspiracy in manner aforesaid.[20]

Dr. Samuel Mudd was a "good" Roman Catholic. He had studied at the Jesuit Georgetown College (now Georgetown University) in Washington. He attended Mass at St. Mary's Church near Bryantown, the spiritual center of the Catholic community or area to which Booth and Herold fled according to the prearranged plan after the assassination.

Dr. Mudd was the physician who set Booth's leg, broken in the jump from Lincoln's box to the stage of the Ford Theatre after the shooting. It was no accident that Booth sought out Dr. Mudd for medical relief. They had schemed together for several months, both in Washington and in Dr. Mudd's home area in Maryland.

SAMUEL ARNOLD: Samuel Arnold was another Roman Catholic, a former student of Georgetown College. The specifications said of him that he "did, within the military department and military lines aforesaid, on or before the 6th day of March, A.D. 1865, and on divers other days and times between that day and the 15th day of April, A.D. 1865, combine, conspire with, and aid, counsel, abet, comfort, and support the said John Wilkes Booth, Lewis

Payne, George A. Atzerodt, Michael O'Laughlin, and their confederates in said unlawful, murderous and traitorous conspiracy, and in the execution thereof aforesaid." [21]

When his parents moved to Baltimore he was tutored by one Rev. J. H. Dashills. Later he was sent to Saint Timothy Hall, Catonsville, Maryland.[22]

MICHAEL O'LAUGHLIN: Michael O'Laughlin was still another Roman Catholic in the group. The indictment before the military tribunal stated that he "did, then and there, lie in wait for Ulysses S. Grant, then Lieutenant General and Commander of the Armies of the United States as aforesaid, with intent, then and there, to kill and murder the said Ulysses S. Grant." [23]

After his death in prison, his body was shipped to Baltimore and buried by his mother in a Catholic cemetery.

EDWARD SPANGLER: Edward Spangler was the most unwitting tool of the conspiracy. He was a theater "stage-door Johnny" and was caught in the web by letting an admired actor into the playhouse and holding his horse while he performed his errand. The court language said that he

> did aid and assist the said John Wilkes Booth to obtain entrance to the box in the said theater, in which said Abraham Lincoln was sitting at the time he was assaulted and shot as aforesaid by John Wilkes Booth; and also did, then and there, aid said Booth in barring and obstructing the door of the box of said theater, so as to hinder and prevent any assistance to, or rescue of, the said Abraham Lincoln against the murderous assault of the said John Wilkes Booth;

## The Hired Hands

and did aid and abet him in making his escape after the said Abraham Lincoln had been murdered in manner aforesaid.[24]

Edward Spangler received the lightest sentence of all those tried. He was not a Roman Catholic.

LOUIS J. WIECHMAN: Louis J. Wiechman (frequently spelled Weichman) knew so much about the detailed ramifications of the Lincoln assassination conspiracy that many feel he may have been more than a witness. He was the principal source of information regarding the ringleaders of the plot.

He, too, was a Roman Catholic. He had studied for the priesthood with John H. Surratt before the War. They remained close friends even after Surratt had become a spy for the Confederacy and Wiechman was working in a Government office in Washington. During the hatching of the conspiracy, Wiechman remained a boarder in Mrs. Surratt's Catholic boarding house.

Henri B. de Ste. Marie, the naturalized American who later discovered Surratt in the Pope's Army, swore in the U.S. Legation in Rome on July 10, 1866, to Rufus King, the U.S. Minister:

> I there and then got acquainted with Louis J. Wiechman and John H. Surratt who came to that locality to pay a visit to the parish priest. At that first interview a great deal was said about the War and slavery—the sentiments expressed by these two individuals being more than strongly secessionists. . . . He (Surratt) then said he was in the secret service of the South, and Wiechman who was in some department there used to steal copies of the dispatches and forward them to him and thence to Richmond.[25]

ANNA WARD: Miss Ward was one of the shadowy characters on the fringe of the conspiracy. Like Wiechman, she may have been more deeply involved than the evidence could prove. She was a Catholic, a teacher in a convent school on G Street in Washington. She was a friend of the Surratt family, was mentioned by witnesses as having been frequently seen in the boarding house. On at least two occasions she delivered coded messages between and for conspirators Booth, John Surratt, and Paine. She seems, in historical perspective, to have been involved more than, for example, Edward Spangler.

On May 1, 1865, Anna Ward's house was searched by orders of the War Department, and she was arrested. Released without trial, she remains one of the mysteries of the Lincoln story.

All of those brought to trial before the military court (the nation was still technically at war when the assassination occurred) were convicted. John H. Surratt had escaped. Booth, of course, had been killed; of this there seems to be no doubt, despite rumors that he escaped and was still alive many years later. Whether he was killed by pursuing troops or, as some historians would prefer to believe, shot himself as the troops set fire to the barn in which he was hiding, is a question that may never be resolved.

The sentences handed down by the court were as follows:

        Mary E. Surratt        Death by hanging
        George A. Atzerodt    Death by hanging

### The Hired Hands

| | |
|---|---|
| David E. Herold | Death by hanging |
| Lewis Paine | Death by hanging |
| Michael O'Laughlin | Life imprisonment |
| Dr. Samuel Mudd | Life imprisonment |
| Samuel Arnold | Life imprisonment |
| Edward Spangler | Six years imprisonment |

To these eight convicted criminals must be added the other two known and proven members of the gang, Booth, the trigger man, and John Surratt, his major accomplice.

Of the ten members of the conspiratorial group, at least seven were Roman Catholics, and the majority of them were good, Mass-attending, practicing Catholics. If the eleventh person, Anna Ward, is included, then not less than eight of the eleven were members of the Catholic Church. Of the others in the plot, only Paine and Spangler had no connections with Catholicism.

However, if the Catholic Church were involved in Lincoln's assassination, its guilt would be no less if none of the hired killers were members of the Faith. But the odds weigh heavily against the "Ancient One" when at least seventy per cent of the villains were her children —at a time when only ten per cent of the people of the United States were claimed by the Hierarchy to be Roman Catholic. In 1865, there were some thirty-five million people in the United States, of whom three and a half million were Catholics.

This fact may give added significance to the words of Brig. Gen. T. M. Harris, a member of the Military Commission which constituted the judges in the trial of the conspirators. One Father Walter, the death row confessor of Mary Surratt, spent twenty-six years after the executions trying to prove her innocent, and as the divine vindication of her guiltlessness, made the absurd and, incidentally, totally false statement that all twelve members of the court, save one, Harris himself, had died miserable deaths. God, in the service of the True Faith, was wreaking His vengeance.

To this Harris, still very much alive, wrote simply:

> Is it not high time that the American people should be fully informed as to this most important episode in their history, in order that they may not be misled by men who were not the friends, but the enemies, of our government in its struggle for its preservation and perpetuation? [26]

Several decades later, the question that Harris posed must again be asked.

Chapter Eight

# The Ancient Privilege of Sanctuary

It is not, nor has it ever been, customary for the Roman Catholic Hierarchy to aid, abet, protect and give asylum to ordinary Catholic criminals. Aside from the ritualistic gestures of "confessing" the condemned, giving them the last rites, or perhaps accompanying them up the "thirteen steps," the Church of Rome has watched generations and centuries of murderers, rapists and unsuccessful political revolutionaries hang, rot in dungeons, or face the firing squads without lifting its pontifical voice, circulating petitions for pardon, or providing an underground for escape.

That is why the extraordinary measures the Catholic Church used to help John H. Surratt, the self-confessed conspirator, escape justice at the end of a rope are so incriminating. The number of priests involved, both in America and in Europe, the open doors of priests' houses, the letters of introduction from priests to priests, from Washington to Montreal, to London, to Paris, to the English (papal) College in Rome, to the Vatican itself—all these condemn the Church as party to Lincoln's assassination as strongly as if Pope Pius IX had signed a confession. The obviously arranged "escape" from the papal army as the American authorities closed in, and the Church's presence and continual interference in Surratt's subsequent trial in Washington, confirm history's verdict of guilt against the Hierarchy.

Nine witnesses testified that they had seen John H. Surratt in Washington on April 14, 1865, the day Lincoln was shot. One Sergeant Dye testified in complete detail —dress, hat, moustache, voice, time of day, etc.—that Surratt was the man in the Ford Theatre who called the signals for Booth to enter the President's box.

Surratt registered in a Montreal hotel on April 18, 1865. He was taken immediately by a Southern sympathizer named Porterfield to his own home. According to a pre-arranged plan, Porterfield took Surratt to his more permanent host, a Catholic priest named Father Boucher. This priest later testified at Surratt's trial that he kept the fugitive, knowing him to be such, at his secluded parish of St. Libore some forty-five miles from Montreal for three months.

Interesting facets in the background and character of Father Boucher were brought out later in John Surratt's trial. The prosecutor, Edwards Pierrepont, was reviewing Boucher's testimony for the jury.

> Well, now Boucher goes on and tells us a little about himself. It was somewhat interesting to know what kind of a man this was that was concealing a person under these false names, and whom he knew to be charged as one of the assassins of the President; at a time, too, when every honorable rebel, when every pagan, and every heathen that heard of it—when the whole civilized world, were sending

# The Ancient Privilege of Sanctuary

expressions of condemnation and letters of condolence to the government. What does he say at such a time as this?

*Q.* Were you in Portland last summer? *A.* I passed through Portland.

*Q.* Did you stop there? *A.* No, sir.

*Q.* Were you at a watering place close by there? *A.* Yes, sir.

*Q.* A place called Cape Elizabeth? *A.* No, sir.

*Q.* Were you at any place near Portland last summer which was a sea watering place? *A.* Yes, sir.

*Q.* What was the name of it? *A.* Old Orchard Beach.

*Q.* How long did you stay there? *A.* About a week.

*Q.* What was the name of the house at which you staid? *A.* I do not remember.

*Q.* Who was there with you that you knew? *A.* Two of the priests.

*Q.* Who were they? *A.* Father Beauregard and Father Hevey.

*Q.* Did you state there that you were his son?

*Mr. Merrick.* Father Beauregard's son?

*Mr. Pierrepont.* Yes, sir.

*Witness.* That is rather a hard question.

Why was it a hard question? What was there hard about it? The simple question was, "Did you state when you were there at that time that you were Father Beauregard's son?"

He is a holy priest in the holy vestments of the church, and the learned counsel called him Father Boucher.

That is rather a hard question, he says. Well, it was hard for him to say that he did, but that was the fact. The next question is, "Did you state at this house that you were his son?" "I do not remember," he answers. Well, I am pretty sure I should never confess to that priest, and I do not believe many people ever will.

Let us read a little further:

*Q.* Did you register your real name? *A.* No, sir.

131

# THE CRIME

*Q.* What name did you register yourself as? *A.* Jary.

*Q.* Did you go there dressed as a priest? *A.* I went dressed as I am now.

*Q.* I ask you if you went there in a Canadian priest's dress? *A.* My answer is, not with the ordinary ecclesiastical suit we wear in Canada—not with the cassock. There is a little difference between the dress in the two countries, and Portland is in the United States.

*Q.* Did you wear the priest's dress of Canada last summer at this watering place? *A.* I was dressed as I am now; you can judge for yourself.

*Mr. Pierrepont.* I have never been in Canada. My question was simply as to whether at this watering place you did wear the Canadian priest's dress? *A.* No, sir.

*Q.* You say you entered a false name on the register? *A.* Yes, sir.

*Q.* Did any difficulty occur there in which you were involved? *A.* Not any to my knowledge.

*Q.* Did you carry yourself or give yourself out there as a priest? *A.* No, sir.

*Q.* What did you call yourself there? *A.* Jary.

*Mr. Pierrepont.* I mean in what character? You say it was not that of a priest? *A.* I did not say what I was.

*Q.* I ask you what you called yourself there in occupation last summer? *A.* If you want me to say what I thought they took me for I can tell you.

*Q.* What? *A.* They took me for a lawyer.

*Q.* Did you disabuse their minds of that? *A.* I did not say anything about it.

*Q.* You did not disabuse their minds of that impression? *A.* No, sir; I thought that was honorable enough.

Suppose, when I get through with this trial, I should go to Canada, and when I got there should dress myself in a priest's apparel and pass myself off as Father So-and-so, and then when I got back here that fact should be disclosed, and when questioned about it I should say, in explanation, "I thought that character of a priest was honorable enough." How would you regard me? You would naturally suspect that some great hidden motive impelled me to this strange course; and so with Father Boucher. If I understand the rule of the Catholic church, it is that the priest shall not put off his dress, shall not take an assumed name, but shall always appear dressed as a holy father, which he professes to be, prepared at all times to hear the confessions of the sinner, to bind up the broken heart and administer the consolations of religion.[1]

The contrast between Father Boucher's moral laxity as to his identity and dress in his secret personal life and his public moral rigidity came out also in the Surratt trial. He was called as a defense witness to discredit Dr. McMillan, who had testified regarding Surratt's confessions of guilt.

It developed that Boucher and McMillan had been feuding for some time. McMillan had been a Catholic but shifted to the Episcopal Church because he would not attend any church (there were two in the area) pastored by Boucher. One source of irritation was ten dollars which the priest owed the doctor and was reluctant to pay. But the principal issue, Boucher said, was a moral doctrine which still alienates Catholic priests and doctors:

> I spoke to him about a principle that I disliked. It was on account of abortion. He argued the point with me, contending that it was not against good morals. I tried to convince him that it was . . . I said to him at that time that I would like to advise him not to practice abortion nor to argue the point before the public; that it would be a great scandal. He then made an insulting reply and I took hold of him by the collar and put him out.[2]

As the "heat" cooled, the priest transferred the fugitive to another of God's representatives, one Father La Pierre. He ensconced the conspirator back in Montreal in a room under the shadow of the bishop. Here Surratt was hidden for two months, or until the Church could arrange passage for him on a boat to England.

The American Government was not unaware of the Church's part in concealing Surratt. The following is an official report: [3]

Mr. Potter to Mr. Seward

(Extracts)

No. 236.  United States Consulate General., B.N.A.P.
Montreal, October 25, 1865

Sir:

I sent a telegram in cipher yesterday informing the department that John H. Surratt left Three Rivers sometime in September for Liverpool, where he now is awaiting the arrival of the steamer Nova Scotian, which sails on Saturday next, by which he expects to receive money from parties in this city, by the hand of ———————— of whom Surratt made a confidant in Liverpool.

I have the information from ————————. It is Surratt's intention to go to Rome. He was secreted at Three Rivers by a Catholic priest there, with whom he lived.

I requested instructions in my telegram, but hearing nothing yet, I scarcely know what course to take. If an officer could proceed to England in this ship, I have no doubt but that Surratt's arrest might be effected, and thus the last of the conspirators against the lives of the President and Secretary of State be brought to justice. If I hear nothing from Washington, I shall go to Quebec tomorrow to see ———————— further on the subject.

## The Ancient Privilege of Sanctuary

  I have the honor to be, very respectfully, your obedient servant,

United States Consul General, B.N.A.P.<br>John F. Potter,

Hon. William H. Seward,
  Secretary of State.

  On September 16, 1865, armed with ecclesiastical introductory letters from the bishop and disguised as McCarthy, he was entrusted to a Dr. McMillen, the ship surgeon of the "Peruvian," bound from Quebec to Liverpool. Both Father Boucher and Father La Pierre, the latter disguised as a layman, had watched over Surratt in a locked stateroom on a shuttle steamer from Montreal to Quebec.[4]

  The monotony of the sea voyage led "McCarthy" into so many confidences with Dr. McMillen that the good doctor reported the whole story to the American Vice-Consul Wilding in Liverpool. Among the details Surratt, who finally told his real name, bragged that once he had carried thirty thousand dollars from Richmond to Canada, again seventy thousand, and also that he and Booth had spent ten thousand dollars in preparation for their plot.[5] When it is recalled that his mother took in boarders for a living, it becomes more evident that Lincoln was not murdered by a handful of mere suicidal patriots.

  The protective network of the Roman Hierarchy again enveloped Surratt when he reached Liverpool. He was ensconced in the Oratory of the Holy Cross, a Roman Catholic institution. Here he was in "sanctuary," the ancient protective privilege of the Church through the Middle Ages. This had been recognized internationally

SURRATT'S FRIGHTFUL LEAP FROM A PRECIPICE WHILE ESCAPING FROM HIS GUARD

## The Ancient Privilege of Sanctuary

for centuries, and still is in some countries, as the inviolate and untouchable refuge of criminals.

United States officials felt they did not yet have enough "evidence of identity and complicity" to have Surratt arrested in a foreign country, but they were keeping an eye on him—and on the Catholic Church, too:[6]

Mr. Wilding to Mr. Seward

(Extracts)

No. 539.                     United States Consulate
                             Liverpool, September 30, 1865.

Sir:

Since my dispatch No. 538, the supposed Surratt has arrived in Liverpool and is now staying at the oratory of the Roman Catholic church of the Holy Cross. His appearance indicates him to be about twenty-one years of age, rather tall, and tolerably good looking.

According to the reports, Mrs. Surratt was a very devout Roman Catholic, and I know that clergymen of that persuasion on their way to and from America have frequently lodged, while in Liverpool, at that same oratory, so that the fact of this young man going there somewhat favors the belief that he is really Surratt.

I can, of course, do nothing further in the matter without Mr. Adams's instructions and a warrant. If it be Surratt, such a wretch ought not to escape.***

Very respectfully, I am, sir, your obedient servant,

H. Wilding.

Hon. William H. Seward,
          Secretary of State.

END OF THE ASSASSIN

## The Ancient Privilege of Sanctuary

By way of Paris, the disguised Surratt, now known as Watson, made his way to Rome where he hid out temporarily in the English College, a Catholic institution for English students. The rector, Father Neane, not only gave him sanctuary but also furnished him money.

His pilgrimage to the Eternal City ended about a year after the murder he had helped to plot, in April of 1866, when he was taken as a soldier into the ninth company of the Zouaves, part of the army of Pope Pius IX.

His guided tour from the Ford Theatre to the protection of the Vatican is summarized in these words by General T. M. Harris:

> He had found friends after his escape from Washington, who had supported him, kept him secreted, watched over his safety, planned his trip from Montreal to Italy, and furnished him money for the expenses of his journey; friends who, no doubt, were accomplices before, as well as after, the fact, for we find them waiting and watching for his return to Montreal after the Assassination, and ready to hurry him off into seclusion. He was to them a stranger; only known to them as a fugitive from his country, charged with the highest crime that a man could commit,—a blow at the nation's life, by murdering the nation's head—a crime against liberty and humanity. These could not have been his friends for personal reasons, but from sympathy in the general purpose of this great crime,—the subversion of our free institutions.[7]

Surratt (Watson) might have slipped into oblivion within the Papal army, had not a former acquaintance, one loyal to the North, also joined the Zouaves. He was Private Henri Benjamin Ste. Marie. On April 21, 1866,

## THE CRIME

he went to Rufus King, the United States Minister, and reported Watson's true identity. Two days later, King informed the State Department in Washington.

Ste. Marie alleged that Surratt was not the only Confederate hiding behind the Pope's robes. When Surratt got drunk, he bragged about the Canadian raids (attacks of arson and pillage by Southern sympathizers and spies based in Canada against Northern cities) and the assassination plot, "greatly to the astonishment and delight of his associates, many of whom were Confederate refugees like himself." [8]

In compliance with instructions from the State Department, Rufus King, on July 14, 1866, forwarded the formal affidavit of Ste. Marie:[9]

Mr. King to Mr. Seward

(Extracts)

No. 59)     Legation of the United States
Rome, July 14, 1866

Sir: * * * * * * In compliance with instructions heretofore received, I have obtained, and herewith transmit, an additional statement, sworn and subscribed to by * * * * * touching J. H. Surratt's acknowledged complicity in the assassination of the late President Lincoln. * * * * again expressed to me his great desire to return to America and give his evidence in person. He thinks that his life would be in danger here, should it be known * * * that he had betrayed Surratt's secret.

I have the honor to be, with great respect, your obedient servant,
                                            Rufus King.

Hon. William H. Seward
        Secretary of State

# The Ancient Privilege of Sanctuary

Hon. William H. Seward
          Secretary of State

                    Rome 10th July 1866

I, Henri de Ste. Marie, a native of Canada, British America, aged thirty three, do swear and declare under oath, that about six months previous to the assassination of President Abraham Lincoln I was living in Maryland, at a small village called Ellen Gowan or Little Texas about twenty five or thirty miles from Baltimore, where I was engaged as teacher, for a period of about five months. I there and then got acquainted with Lewis J. Wiechman and John H. Surratt, who came to that locality to pay a visit to the parish priest.

At that first interview a great deal was said about the war and slavery—the sentiments expressed by these two individuals being more than strongly secessionists. In the course of the conversation I remember Surratt to have said that President Lincoln would certainly pay for all the men that were slain during the war. About a month after I removed to Washington at the instigation of Wiechman and got a situation as Tutor in St. Mathew's Institute, where he was himself engaged, Surratt visited us weekly, and once he offered me to send me South, but I declined. I did not remain more than one month at Washington, not being able to agree with Wiechman and enlisted in the army of the North as stated in my first statement in writing to General King.

I have met Surratt here in Italy at a small town called Velletri, he is now known under the name of John Watson, I recognized him before he made himself known to me, and told him privately: "You are John Surratt, the person I have known in Maryand." He acknowledged he was and begged of me to keep the thing secret. After some conversation, we spoke of the unfortunate affair of the assassination of President Lincoln, and these were his words "Damn the Yankees, they have killed my mother, but I have done them as much

## THE CRIME

harm as I could, we have killed Lincoln, the niggers' friend." He then said speaking of his mother: "Had it not been for me and that coward Wiechman my mother would be living yet. It was fear made him speak, had he kept his tongue there was no danger for him, but if I ever return to America or meet him elsewhere, I shall kill him." He then said he was in the secret service of the South, and Wiechman who was in some department there used to steal copies of the dispatches and forward them to him and thence to Richmond. Speaking of the murder he said they had acted under the orders of men who are not yet known, some of whom are still in New York and others in London, I am aware that money is sent him yet from London. When I left Canada he said, I had but little money but I had a letter for a party in London, I was in disguise, with dyed hair and false beard, that party sent me to a Hotel where he told me to remain till I would hear from him, after a few weeks he came and proposed me to go to Spain, but I declined and asked to go to Paris, he gave me Seventy pounds with a letter of introduction to a party there, who sent him here to Rome, where he joined the Zouaves, he says he can get money in Rome at any time.

I believe he is protected by the Clergy and that the murder is the result of a deep laid plot not only against the life of President Lincoln, but against the existence of the republic, as we are aware that priesthood and royalty are and always have been opposed to liberty. That such men as Surratt, Booth, Wiechman and others, should of their own accord plan and execute the infernal plot which resulted in the death of President Lincoln is impossible. There are others behind the curtain who have pulled the strings to make these scoundrels act.

I have also asked him if he knew Jefferson Davis he said no, but that he had acted under the instructions of persons under his immediate orders, being asked if Jefferson Davis had anything to do with the assassination he said "I am not going to tell you." My impression is that he brought the order from Richmond, as he was in the habit of going there weekly, he must have bribed the others to do it, for when the event took place he told me he was in New York, prepared to fly as soon as the deed would be done. He says that he does not regret what has taken place, and that he will visit New York in a year or two, as there is a heavy shipping firm there, who had much to do with the South, and he is surprised that they have not been suspected.

This is the exact truth of what I know about Surratt, more I could not learn being afraid to awaken his suspicions.

And furthermore I do not say.

Henri B. de Ste. Marie

Sworn and subscribed before me at the American Legation in Rome this tenth (10th) day of July A.D. 1866.

Rufus King
Minister Resident

The United States had no extradition treaty with the Papal States. Therefore, Rufus King, on orders from Secretary of State Seward, requested rather than demanded, that Surratt be released to American authorities. The Vatican, regardless of its proven sympathies for the South, did not dare openly refuse the victorious United States Government.

Nevertheless, Cardinal Antonelli informed Rufus King that the Papal Government hesitated to release the man because "capital punishment (which was) likely to ensue was not exactly in accordance with the spirit of the Papal Government." [10]

This sanctimonious front of the Vatican is ludicrous,

## THE CRIME

not only against the backdrop of the historic attitude of the Popes toward mere heretics, not murderers, especially during the blood-drenched centuries of the Papal Inquisition, but also in light of the personal behavior of Pius IX toward his political enemies. He not only cursed them and excommunicated ninety-eight per cent of the Italian people (Encyclical "Respicientes"), but stuffed his prisons with them, chained them to the walls, and quite freely and blithely executed them.

Under the prodding of Rufus King, Cardinal Antonelli ordered the arrest of Surratt. This was done at Veroli near Rome, and the Pontifical Commander promised to conduct the prisoner safely to Rome.

Then occurred the comic opera events of this whole tragic story. Surratt, escorted by six guards, asked to use a primitive army latrine which had been constructed protruding over a ravine one hundred feet deep. The guards permitted him to do so—alone. He jumped through a window, down the sheer wall, and into the filth below. Fifty Zouaves rushed in hot pursuit—and couldn't catch him.[11]

Surratt made his way to Naples and, under the name of John Agostina, boarded a ship for Egypt. There United States Consul-General Charles Hale captured him, even though he insisted that his name was Walters. Hale wired the State Department, "Have arrested John Surratt, one of President Lincoln's assassins. No doubt of identity."[12]

Chapter Nine

# The Trial of John Surratt

"Now, gentlemen of the jury, I have proved, first, the existence of this conspiracy; secondly, the object of it, which was, if you believe the testimony of Mrs. McClermont, to murder, and which, original object the result showed, was persistently adhered to.

"The change in the plan of their operations, to which Booth alluded when he wrote to Surratt in the city of Montreal, was not from abduction to murder, but from the telescopic rifle to the cup, to the pistol, to the dagger. It was murder at first; it was murder in the interim; it was murder to the last. I argued out of abundant caution, that even if it were not so, if he continued a member of the conspiracy up to the time of the consummation of its purpose, he was guilty of murder, if the result was the violent death of the victim whom they had selected for the gratification of their malice.

"Having, then, shown him here, in addition to these facts, I next proceed to show you the part he did perform in this bloody tragedy, although it is not essential to the case, for, as I have told you, if he performed any part, however minute, he is guilty of the whole."

From summation of prosecutor
Edwards Pierrepont to the Surratt jury.[1]

## THE CRIME

The trial of John Surratt was an anticlimax in the drama of the assassination of Abraham Lincoln. It began June 10, 1867, more than two years after the murder of "our martyred hero."

Rebel Southern partisans and sympathizers were no longer an enemy class apart. Except for the diehards who had crossed the Mexican border to fight on as mercenaries, or who had travelled westward with wagon trains to become half-outlaws, or those who, like Surratt, had concealed themselves in the armies of the Pope, the defeated were gradually becoming integrated into American civil life. They were granted citizenship rights despite the fact that they had borne arms against their Government, and they were permitted to sit on juries—even on a jury trying a man accused of murdering the President of the United States.

But if the history of Surratt's trial points up the fact that Confederate sympathy blocked justice toward a proven conspirator—as it certainly did—it also demonstrates conclusively the great interest in the welfare of a coward, conspirator, and traitor on the part of his fellow-Catholics, and particularly their Jesuit priests. That the influence exerted in Surratt's behalf came from the ecclesiastical superiors of these priests, again especially the Jesuits, is inherent in the monolithic structure of the Church.

Cardinal Antonelli and Pope Pius IX were still alive when John Surratt went to trial. The Papal States of the "Ancient One" had not yet crumbled before the armies of King Victor Emmanuel II. The first Vatican Ecumenical Council was *in petto,* in the making. This was the

Council which, two years after Surratt's trial, was to declare Pius IX infallible, thus locking the Roman Catholic world forever into the vise of mental totalitarianism, the proposition from which Abraham Lincoln had dedicated his life to free mankind.

Before and after the assassination, Surratt had been well supplied with money. There have been two plausible explanations of the sources of these funds. One was the Confederacy. But now the Confederacy no longer existed. Its currency was useless. Its resources were gone.

Surratt himself now had no money. His lawyers presented what was the equivalent of a modern pauper's oath:

> To the Honorable, the Justices of the Supreme Court of the District of Columbia, holding the Criminal Court in March Term, 1867.
>
> The petition of John H. Surratt shows that he has been put upon his trial in a capital case in this court; that he has exhausted all his means, and such further means as have been furnished him by the liberality of his friends, in preparing for his defense, and he is now unable to procure the attendance of his witnesses. He therefore prays your Honor for an order that process may issue to summon his witnesses, and to compel their attendance at the cost of the government of the United States, according to the statute in such cases made and provided.[2]

Yet Surratt had three defense lawyers: R. T. Merrick, Joseph H. Bradley, and Joseph H. Bradley, Jr., of whom at least the first was a Catholic. Who chose them? Who paid them? Surratt's case was not the popular defense of a martyr that the Legal Aid Society would assume as a

# THE REPORTER,

### A Periodical Devoted to Religion, Law, Legislation, and Public Events.

## SPEECH TO THE JURY

OF

## RICHARD T. MERRICK, ESQ.,

ON THE

## TRIAL OF JOHN H. SURRATT,

IN THE

### SUPREME COURT OF THE DISTRICT OF COLUMBIA,

SITTING FOR THE TRIAL OF CRIMES AND MISDEMEANORS,

ON AN INDICTMENT FOR

## Murder of President Lincoln,

BEFORE HIS HONOR GEORGE P. FISHER,

One of the Justices of the Supreme Court for the District of Columbia.

*Commencing Monday, June 10, 1867.*

---

### ARGUMENT FOR THE DEFENCE.

R. SUTTON,
WASHINGTON CITY, D. C.
1867.

McGill & Withrow, Printers and Stereotypers, Washington, D. C.

## The Trial of John Surratt

public charity. What group of lawyers would donate their services for fifty-five days of trial in addition to five months of preparation?

A point that has never been clarified was the amount paid for defense witnesses. Surratt had filed a pauper's oath and requested compensation of his witnesses by the Government. Yet one Canadian witness for Surratt, Alexis Burnette, testified that another, one Sarsfield B. Nagle, had told him that he had already received $500.00 in gold "for services, fees and expenses." [3] The testimony was not questioned or denied by Surratt's attorneys. When it is recalled that there were one hundred and twenty-one witnesses for Surratt, a sizable sum is involved. Where did it come from?

The grand jury of Washington, D.C., had indicted John Surratt on four technical counts: (1) that John H. Surratt murdered Abraham Lincoln on April 14, 1865; (2) that John H. Surratt and John Wilkes Booth did "make an assault" on Abraham Lincoln and that Booth accomplished the murder; (3) that Surratt and all the other conspirators "did make an assault" on Lincoln, and he was murdered by Booth; (4) that Surratt and the others "did unlawfully and wickedly combine, confederate and conspire and agree together feloniously to kill and murder" Lincoln, and that Booth accomplished the deed "in pursuance of said unlawful and wicked conspiracy."

From the first moment of his return to the United States after having been concealed in the Vatican sanctuary, Surratt's trial shows evidence of the continued effort of the Church on his behalf. Of twenty-six men called for the jury panel, sixteen were Roman Catholics. Could this have been an accident or a coincidence? The authorities themselves did not think so. Whereas sixty-two per cent of the panel was Catholic, only ten per cent of the population adhered to that faith.

The Washington reporter of the *Saturday Evening Gazette* of Boston congratulated Judge Fisher on throwing out the whole panel:

> ... that the (first) panel of twenty-six men was largely Irish Catholic and Democratic, the bare calling of their names gave assurance to everybody. The chief objection thereto, it seemed to me, lay in the fact that it was a panel of dunces. Not one face in six, of the two benches full, was that of a man ordinarily intelligent. I am utterly at a loss to understand how it was possible, without extra effort, to get together such a company of stupids. Whether it be possible to secure conviction, whatever the testimony, before a jury composed in large part of Catholics, is a question as to which there may be differences of opinion; but as it is especially desirable that this case, involving the great mystery of the assassination conspiracy, should be tried before intelligent men, I think it a case of congratulation that the judge grant(ed) the motion of the district attorney.[4]

Judge Fisher, in ordering a new panel selected, summarized his opinion:

> Believing, therefore, that the substantial requirements of the act of Congress in this case providing for the selection of a fair and impartial jury, have not been complied with, entirely set at naught, and that there has been grave default on the part of the officers whom that act has substituted in the place of the marshal, for the purpose of having them exercise a united judgment in the selection of all the persons whose names are to go in the jury box, I am constrained to

> allow the motion of challenge in this case. I do not consider the fact that the present panel were improperly drawn by the clerk of Georgetown, who had no right to put his hand into the box, *because the objection which I have allowed lies even deeper than that.* It is, therefore, ordered by the Court that the present panel be set aside, and that the Marshal of the District of Columbia do now proceed to summon a jury of talesmen.[5]

The abnormal preoccupation of the Roman Catholic clergy with the protection and release of John Surratt continued throughout the trial. An eyewitness observed that Jesuit priests were so conspicuous in daily attendance at the sessions that it seemed they had been ordered to be present to impress the jury. Many of the defense witnesses were Catholic.[6]

A study of the transcript of the trial certainly verifies this point. Particularly of interest were the Canadians called to break down the veracity of Ste. Marie, who had discovered Surratt in the Papal Army. They all showed sympathy for the Confederacy and claimed Ste. Marie was untruthful. Their testimony was all similar to that of Sarsfield B. Nagle, a law graduate of St. Mary's Jesuit School in Montreal, that Ste. Marie, in exposing Surratt to the U.S. Government, was "mean, unprincipled, and an informer."[7]

A Father John Menu, a teacher at St. Charles College, spent much time sitting with Surratt and with vacationing Catholic students who attended the trial, pointedly shaking hands with the prisoner.[8]

The prosecution lawyers painstakingly kept Roman Catholic Church implications out of their examinations, cross-examinations, and arguments. Their caution is shown in their spontaneous attempt to stop Surratt's Catholic attorney, Merrick, from discrediting the prosecution witness Sgt. Jos. M. Dye because of his religion. Dye had testified at great length of Surratt's presence with Booth at the Ford Theatre just before the assassination:

> *Merrick*: Q. What is your religious faith? A. I am a Protestant.
> Q. Of what denomination?
> *Pierrepont*: I must object to that.
> *Merrick*: I will waive the question. I thought it possible he was a Swedenborgian.
> *Mr. Pierrepont*: We don't desire to bring religion into this case in any way.
> *District Attorney (E. C. Carrington)*: I have no objection to the witness disclosing his religion but we object upon principle to introducing any religious inquisition into a court of justice.
> *Merrick*: I have no purpose to introduce religious inquisition, nor to follow your example in any particular.
> *District Attorney*: I think that remark is entirely without foundation.[9]

Because of this caution, the reader of the transcript a century after the trial cannot refrain from sharing the indignation and surprise felt by General Harris, a member of the military tribunal which had presided at the 1865 trial of the other conspirators, and a witness at Surratt's trial. He wrote:

> Mr. Merrick, however, seized the occasion to pass an eulogium on that church, in which he showed as much disregard for the facts of history as he did for the proven facts in this case. Perhaps he felt this vindication to be called for from the fact that most of the conspirators were

## The Trial of John Surratt

Catholics in religion, and the further fact that the friends who waited and watched for the return of his client to Montreal after the assassination, and who, on his return, spirited him away and kept him secreted for five months and then helped him off to Italy, where he was found in the ranks of the Pope's army, and who voluntarily came before the court on his trial to testify, and to procure testimony in his behalf, were priests of that church.

In his eulogium on that church he forgot to mention the fact that the Pope at an early period of the war acknowledged the Southern Confederacy and wrote a sympathizing letter to Jefferson Davis, in which he called him his dear son and denounced President Lincoln as a tyrant. He could scarcely have forgotten that the Pope of Rome had sought to take advantage of the arduous struggle in which our government was engaged for the preservation of its life, to establish a Catholic Empire in Mexico, and had sent Maximilian, a Catholic prince, to reign over that, at that time, unhappy people, under the protection of the arms of France, lent to the furtherance of his unholy purpose by the last loyal son of the church, that ever occupied a throne in Europe. Perhaps he did not realize that it was God who frustrated that last grasp of the drowning man at a straw that eluded his grasp, by preparing for his holiness, the Pope, and for Louis Napoleon just at that moment the Franco-Prussian war, which resulted in the final loss of his temporal power to the Pope and with it his grip on the world, and of his empire and crown to the last servile supporter of his temporal pretensions.

To claim for that church, as Mr. Merrick did, friendship to civil liberty, respect for the rights of conscience and of private judgment, and love of our republican institutions, is to ignore, or set at naught, all the dogmas of that church on the above questions and all the claims of the Papacy. Mr. Merrick manifestly thought that the attitude of the Catholic clergy toward the assassination of the President could be hidden from public view by his fulsome eulogy.[10]

## THE CRIME

In his argument to the jury, Surratt's Catholic attorney, R. T. Merrick, suddenly broke off his emotional portrayal of Mrs. Surratt's "nameless felon's grave" with the following pointless interlude, to which Harris refers:

> Gentlemen, something has been said in the earlier part of this case with regard to the Catholic Church, and her connection with the prisoner at the bar and the Southern Confederacy. She needs no vindication from me. There she stands, and there is her history. Whether her children believe the church of God, or, as other men, believe the devices of man, she there stands, one of the grandest institutions that the world has ever beheld. She guided men from darkness to civilization, and through the whole period of despotic authority in Europe she has been upon the side of the people, and against monarchy. From the first beginning of her power she has upheld the rights of the people whenever oppression has attempted to violate law; and whenever the people have been turbulent in their resistance to legitimate authority she has restrained them by the mandate of her spiritual power to respect the law and obey the constituted authorities of their country. And in our late rebellion she said to all people, north and south, "Obey the law, and respect the Constitution of your country. I speak not politics," says she, "in my church. The banner which is floating from this church is the banner of the cross in all countries; and as the follower of the Cross, I teach all people to obey the law." Such was her conduct with regard to our late rebellion. Such she stands forth to her eternal credit; and throughout her history, even to those who question the divinity of her origin, there is much that is too great for the machinations of men, and they stand almost confessing what their judgment and feelings question. . . . To the honor of the Catholic Church be it said; that when this young man was accused of crime in the papal dominions, and there was no extradition treaty between this country and that, and no

> power to compel the Pope to surrender him, the Pope and Cardinal Antonelli voluntarily, and without hesitation, gave him up. They said, "Take him back to America and try him; if guilty, execute him." The Catholic Church is on the side of virtue and mercy. She protects the fleeing criminal when she believes him to be innocent, but when the hand of power says, "he is guilty, give him to me," she gave him up without a word.[11]

Evidently the Catholic Merrick had not read the recent encyclical, *Incredibili Afflictamur* (1863) in which Pope Pius had simply abolished the laws and constitution of Colombia, nor was he keeping up with current events in Italy, where the same Pope Pius was even then excommunicating, imprisoning, and killing his fellow Italians who were fighting for democratic freedom against his papal monarchy.

Much of the testimony on both sides was a rehash of that given at the original trial of the other conspirators. The defense tried to play on the heartstrings of the jury, making powerful, sympathetic funereal harmony out of the "innocence" of Surratt's mother and the fact that her "mouldering remains" lay in the unmarked grave of a criminal, and that a cruel heartless government would not give what was left of that "mortal coil" to Surratt's sister Anna to keep her from becoming completely insane with grief.

Surratt had admitted being a paid Confederate spy, and it was conclusively established that he was a close associate of all of the conspirators. The government brought forth a preponderance of evidence to prove that he was in Washington on the day of the Lincoln murder.

**THE CRIME**

The defense tried to prove that he was in Elmira, New York on that day.

Through the hot and sticky days of June, July, and early August, the jury heard eight-five witnesses for the prosecution with ninety-six for the Government's rebuttal, ninety-eight for the defense with twenty-three for its rebuttal—a total of three hundred and two.

In that air of legal confusion, partisan and religious undertones, and intolerable weather, it is understandable that the jury could not have agreed on convicting anyone. The jury was hung and proposed to stay that way. Judge Fisher discharged it in despair.

A second attempt at trial was made but failed. John H. Surratt was released on $40,000 bond—an astronomical sum at the time. On September 22, 1868, a plea was filed on his behalf on the grounds that he, like the leaders of the Confederacy, was included in the general pardon issued by President Andrew Johnson on July 4, 1868. The case against him was dismissed November 5, 1868.

In the anticlimactic years of his life, John Surratt worked at many things, including an unsuccessful fling at the lecture platform. Sometime between 1870 and 1872, the Roman Catholic Church again showed an interest in him. He was hired as a teacher in St. Joseph Catholic School in Emmitsburg, Maryland. The school was located in the Fireman's Hall directly opposite St. Joseph's Catholic Church.

John H. Surratt died Friday, April 21, 1916. A student at Georgetown University, writing a biased whitewash of the role of the Church in the entire Surratt case, described the funeral as being:

## The Trial of John Surratt

held on the following Monday from his home on 1004 West Lanvale Street, Baltimore. A Solemn High Requiem Mass was offered at St. Pius Church by the pastor, the Rev. John E. Dunn, and John Harrison Surratt was laid to rest in Bonnie Brae Cemetery.[12]

It was indeed a fitting end, a final and significant touch. For as every priest and many observant laymen know, a Solemn High Requiem Mass, with three priests officiating (that is what the words mean) is usually reserved for the funerals of bishops, priests, or nuns.

The Solemn High Requiem Mass is not offered for ordinary spies, any more than for the sons of ordinary bartenders. When it is chanted at the funeral services of a layman, it is as a token of recognition and appreciation for exceptional devotion or distinguished service to the Church.

It was done for John Harrison Surratt. It must have been deserved.

Chapter Ten

# Epilogue

Speculation as to the person or organization behind the bullet that cut down America's hero of freedom may seem not only endless but also useless. After all, he has been dead for a century, and all of his possible enemies have long since joined him.

But if that bullet represented anything more than fanatic frenzy, the search might have meaning to us who are the heirs to his bequest of freedom.

A recapitulation could well start with a list of all the suspects and the elimination of the impossible individuals or groups:

1. John Wilkes Booth, alone.
2. A group of wholly independent, self-appointed, dedicated fanatics. This would comprise Booth, Mary Surratt, Dr. Mudd, Artzerodt, Paine, Herold, O'Laughlin, and Spangler, and the others tried and convicted, together with John Surratt, accused, indicted, and finally granted amnesty.
3. Booth, alone or with his group of conspirators, working as agents of Vice-President Andrew Johnson.

### Epilogue

4. The same person or persons, working on behalf of Secretary of War Edwin McMasters Stanton.
5. The Confederacy, either by order of Jefferson Davis alone, or through the Southern Cabinet, or jointly through the Southern Cabinet and collaborators in Canada—the so-called "Canadian Cabinet."
6. The Roman Catholic Church, either directly through the indicted conspirators, Booth and company, or indirectly, by using the Southern groups.

Some of these possibilities can easily be eliminated.

John Wilkes Booth as a lone assassin? This theory is ruled out merely by the fact that Lincoln's assassination was to be accompanied by the simultaneous murder of Vice-President Johnson, Secretary of State William Seward, and General Ulysses S. Grant.

A mutually self-appointed, dedicated group of fanatics? There can be no question about the fact that Booth, the Surratts, and Dr. Mudd were dedicated. They were also sincere in their beliefs that Lincoln was the enemy of the South and of the society they wished to perpetuate. But the exclusiveness of their operations is disproven by the official connection of John Surratt with the Confederacy, both in Richmond and in Canada; by the large amount of money that flowed so freely from them and among them; by the determined efforts to defend them and protect them after the assassination.

Vice-President Andrew Johnson? It is inconceivable that Johnson would cover his part in the scheme by planning his own assassination. It has been argued that Johnson's motive was jealousy of Lincoln. He may have been jealous, but his general ineptitude, as proven by the later impeachment proceedings against him, made him incapable of planning or executing a plot as daring and devious as the murder of his Commander-in-Chief, and as incredible as his own elimination!

Secretary of War Stanton? The motives attributed to Stanton are various and contradictory. Tokens of evidence against him are also various. They include the lack of military protection for Lincoln at the Ford Theatre on April 14th; the withdrawing of the soldiers from the Washington escape routes, especially the bridge across the Potomac, on that same night; the alleged vindictive "persecution" of Mary Surratt; the cancellation of the reward for the capture of John H. Surratt.

It would require an extensive book to analyze these and other charges against this strong and controversial figure. This now exists in the comprehensive volume "Stanton," by Benjamin P. Thomas and Harold M. Hyman. Exhaustive detail on Stanton's actions can also be found in the official Executive Documents of the House of Representatives, Second Session of the Thirty-Ninth Congress, 1866-1867. The work of Thomas and Hyman and the official Congressional documents leave little doubt that Stanton neither plotted, aided, abetted, nor approved the murder of his Commander-in-Chief.

The Confederacy? That the leaders of the South were implicated in conspiracies regarding the person of Abraham Lincoln, either by the kidnapping or by the murder of the Presdent, or possibly by both, can hardly be questioned. That they *alone* were involved is the question of this book. In fact it is the thesis of this book that they

### Epilogue

did not alone consummate the assassination. They could not have done it. The actual murder took place after their cause was hopelessly lost and when they had already surrendered. Furthermore, the spiriting away, the concealment, and the legal defense of one of the principal conspirators took place *after* the Confederacy had *ceased to exist.*

There was one group, one organization, whose historical background was characterized by the planning and execution of such deeds; that had a lasting consistent motive, before, during and after the crime; that had the necessary international connections; that had the money; that could elicit suicidal self-sacrifice in its members; and that continued to exist through all phases of the assassination conspiracy. This is the Roman Catholic Church.

A recapitulation of the evidence already presented will bear out these points:

* The sympathies of Northern Irish Catholics (i.e., the bulk of American Catholics) were for the continued slavery of the Negro and strongly against Lincoln.
* In the War with Mexico, some Irish Catholics preferred their Church to their nation and deserted to Mexico.
* Irish Catholics created the Draft Riots of New York City which dangerously jeopardized the cause of Lincoln. Archbishop Hughes of New York betrayed Lincoln by doing nothing to stop the Riots.
* The Church had developed a theoretical justification for the murder of heretics, and to the Church Lincoln was a heretic.
* The Church had for centuries been involved in numerous instances of the forcible removal of heads of state whom it condemned, and had been implicated on many occasions

## THE CRIME

in conspiracy to commit regicide and related acts of assassination.
* The Church considered Abraham Lincoln a major enemy, not only because of such specific incidents as his eloquent and brilliant defense of the ex-priest Chiniquy, but also because of his opposition to Church influence in the New World.
* Pope Pius IX repeatedly condemned the principles of American democracy and freedom as being unacceptable and dangerous to the very existence of Roman Catholicism. Abraham Lincoln was the living personification of these principles.
* During Lincoln's presidency, Pius IX issued the autocratic, totalitarian Syllabus of Errors, which "infallibly" condemned the basic principles of American Government. He also during these same years attempted to crush the rise of freedom, especially religious freedom, in Mexico, Colombia, Austria and, with excommunication, imprisonment and death, in Italy.
* The scheme of Napoleon III, Emperor Franz Joseph, and Pope Pius IX to put Maximilian on a throne in Mexico included the plan to absorb the South and ultimately the North when Lincoln was defeated.
* The Vatican's well-known sympathy for the South throughout the early part of the War was echoed in the sympathy and action among the Jesuits in Rome and America, and among the Irish in Ireland and in the North.
* The plot to assassinate Lincoln was "hatched" in a Roman Catholic home by adherents of the Church. The escape plan of the conspirators centered in a Roman Catholic neighborhood, again among adherents of the Church.
* At least sixty per cent of the actual immediate conspirators were Roman Catholics.
* John H. Surratt, the only escaping principal conspirator, was hidden in Canada by Catholic priests, sent to England by Catholic priests, hidden in London by Catholic priests

### Epilogue

in a Catholic rectory, and concealed in Rome by Catholic priests in a Catholic College.
* John H. Surratt was hidden out in the Zouave Army of Pope Pius IX under an assumed name.
* John H. Surratt was defended, long after the Confederacy had disintegrated, in a very extended and expensive trial, by a firm of attorneys whose most active participant was a Roman Catholic.
* John H. Surratt received the active sympathy, throughout his trial, of Roman Catholic priests and the students of the St. Charles College.
* John H. Surratt was hired, after being included in the general amnesty, by Catholic priests to teach in a Roman Catholic school in the United States, although he had never been exonerated of the crime to murder the President of the United States.

Reading history for history's sake is no more productive than reading fairy tales. The history of the past is useless if it teaches us nothing of the future. Regardless of advancing science and instantaneous communication the mania of man for power over mankind is no different in 1963 than it was in the day of Osiris, Nebuchadnezzar, Alexander the Great, Julius Caesar, Charlemagne, Genghis Khan, Elizabeth I, Adolph Hitler, or Pope Pius IX.

The Papacy is just as totalitarian in the nineteen sixties as it was a century ago. The Jesuit vow is, if anything, even more rigid. The Vatican still makes concordats with any nation it can intimidate. It made them with Hitler and Mussolini. It has these freedom-destroying compacts in 1963 with Italy, Spain, Portugal, and Colombia.

Roman Catholic writers, priests, cardinals, apostolic delegates, and popes work as frantically and frenetically to absorb men's minds and their fortunes as when Napoleon III, Franz Joseph, Maximilian, and Pope Pius IX schemed in Vienna, Paris, Miramar, and Rome to take over North America.

The teachings of the Church on freedom of thought, of speech, of writing and of worship have not changed since Abraham Lincoln took office. In 1864, primitive communications made the diffusion of the Syllabus of Errors slow and difficult. Now it is in paperback on the nation's newsstands.

In Lincoln's day the Vatican had 3,500,000 adherents in the United States; now it claims 43,000,000. Then it had 46 dioceses; now it has 140. Then it had a fragmentary Church press; now it has 506 publications with 27,560,781 subscriptions. Then it had a handful of children in a handful of schools; now it has almost 6,000,000 students in 13,278 schools.

In 1865 it conspired against the American pattern of "live and let live" amid the secrecy of Mrs. Surratt's boarding house. Today, its cardinals and bishops openly press their unconstitutional demands for tax subsidy of their schools in the halls of Congress. Through the fearful threat of boycott they seek to silence as "bigoted," "anti-Catholic" or "prejudiced" any independent opposition by the press, radio, television, or by businessmen. They force theatres to reject motion pictures that are critical, and even try to ban them in Masonic Temples and Shrine Auditoriums.

In 1865 a man was assassinated. In 1963 the free human mind is being assassinated. In the world of ideas and principles, only "a strong man, armed, keepeth his court."

# APPENDIX

# Excerpts from the Words of Two Men

### Abraham Lincoln

I have never had a feeling politically that did not spring from the sentiments embodied in the Declaration of Independence. . . . I have often inquired of myself what great principle or idea it was that kept the Confederacy so long together. It was not the mere matter of the separation of the Colonies from the motherland; but that sentiment in the Declaration of Independence which gave liberty, not alone to the people of this country, but, I hope, to the world, for all future time. It was that which gave promise that in due time the weight would be lifted from the shoulders of all men. This is the sentiment embodied in the Declaration of Independence. Now, my friends, can this country be saved upon that basis? If it can, I will consider myself one of the happiest men in the world, if I can help to save it. If it cannot be saved upon that principle, it will be truly awful. But if this country cannot be saved without giving up that principle, I was about to say I would rather be assassinated on this spot than surrender it.

*Independence Hall, Philadelphia,*
*February 22, 1861*

# Appendix

### Pope Pius IX

Our predecessors have, with apostolic fortitude, continually resisted the machinations of those evil men, who, 'foaming out their own confusion, like the raging waves of the sea', and 'promising liberty, while they are themselves the slaves of corruption', endeavored by their fallacious opinions and most wicked writings to subvert the foundations of Religion and of civil Society, to remove from our midst all virtue and justice, to deprave the hearts and minds of all, to turn away from right discipline of morals the incautious, and especially inexperienced youth, miserably corrupting them, leading them into the nets of error, and finally withdrawing them from the bosom of the Catholic Church. . . . These false and perverse opinions are so much the more detestable, by as much as they have chiefly for their object to hinder and banish that salutary influence which the Catholic Church, by the institution and command of her Divine Author, ought freely to exercise, even to the consummation of the world, not only over invidual men, but nations, peoples, and sovereigns.

*Encyclical "Quanta Cura,"*
*December 8, 1864*

### Pope Pius IX

ERROR #47. The best theory of civil society requires that popular schools open to children of every class of the people, and, generally, all public institutes intended for instruction in letters and philosophical sciences and for carrying on the education of youth, should be freed from all ecclesiastical authority, control and interference, and should be fully subjected to the civil and political power at the pleasure of the

## Appendix

rulers, and according to the standard of the prevalent opinions of the age.

*Syllabus of Errors,
December 8, 1864*

### Abraham Lincoln

The doctrine of self-government is right—absolutely and eternally right.

*Speech at Peoria, Illinois (reply to Douglas),
October 16, 1854*

### Abraham Lincoln

Upon the subject of education, not presuming to dictate any plan or system respecting it, I can only say that I view it as the most important subject which we as a people can be engaged in. That every man may receive at least a moderate education, and thereby be enabled to read the histories of his own and other countries, by which he may duly appreciate the value of our free institutions, appears to be an object of vital importance, even on this account alone, to say nothing of the advantages and satisfaction to be derived from all being able to read the scriptures and other works, both of a religious and moral nature, for themselves. For my part, I desire to see the time when education, and by its means, morality, sobriety, enterprise and industry, shall become much more general than at present, and should be gratified to have it in my power to contribute something to the advancement of any measure which might have a tendency to accelerate the happy period.

*To people of Sagamo County,
March 9, 1832*

**Appendix**

## Pope Pius IX

ERROR #55. The Church ought to be separated from the State, and the State from the Church.

*Syllabus of Errors,
December 8, 1864*

## Pope Pius IX

Teach them 'that kingdoms rest upon the foundation of the Catholic faith, and that nothing is so deadly, nothing so certain to engender every ill, nothing so exposed to danger, as for men to believe that they stand in need of nothing else than the free will which we received at birth, if we ask nothing further from the Lord; that is to say, if, forgetting our Author, we abjure His power to show that we are free.' And do not omit to teach, 'that the royal power has been established, not only to exercise the government of the world, but, above all, for the protection of the Church; and that there is nothing more profitable and more glorious for the Sovereigns of States, and Kings, than to leave the Catholic Church to exercise her laws, and not to permit any to curtail her liberty;' as our most wise and courageous Predecessor, St. Felix, wrote to the Emperor Zeno. 'It is certain that it is advantageous for Sovereigns, when the cause of God is in question, to submit their Royal will, according to his ordinance, to the Priests of Jesus Christ, and not to prefer it before them.

*Encyclical "Quanta Cura,"
December 8, 1864*

## Abraham Lincoln

What I do say is that no man is good enough to govern another man *without that other's consent.* I say this is the

### Appendix

leading principle—the sheet anchor of American republicanism. Our Declaration of Independence says:

> "We hold these truths to be self evident: That all men are created equal; that they are endowed by their Creator with certain inalienable rights; that among these are life, liberty and the pursuit of happiness. That to secure these rights, governments are instituted among men, DERIVING THEIR JUST POWERS FROM THE CONSENT OF THE GOVERNED."

Finally, I insist that if there is ANYTHING which it is the duty of the WHOLE PEOPLE to never entrust to any hands but their own, that thing is the preservation and perpetuity of their own liberties and institutions.

*Reply to Senator Douglas, Peoria, Ill., October 16, 1854*

#### Pope Pius IX

ERROR #45. The entire government of public schools in which the youth of a Christian state is educated, except (to a certain extent) in the case of episcopal seminaries, may and ought to appertain to the civil power, and belong to it so far that no other authority whatsoever shall be recognized as having any right to interfere in the discipline of the schools, the arrangement of the studies, the conferring of degrees, in the choice or approval of the teachers.

*Syllabus of Errors, December 8, 1864*

#### Pope Pius IX

From this totally false notion of social government, they fear not to uphold that erroneous opinion most pernicious to the Catholic Church, and to the salvation of souls, which was called by Our Predecessor, Gregory XIV, the insanity (deliramentum): namely, 'that the liberty of conscience and of worship is the peculiar (or inalienable) right of every man, which should be proclaimed by law, and that citizens have the right to all kinds of liberty, by which they may be enabled to manifest openly and publicly their ideas, by word of mouth, through the press, or by any other means.' But whilst these men make these rash assertions, they do not reflect, or consider, that they preach the liberty of perdition, and that, 'if it is always free to human arguments to discuss, men will never be wanting who will dare to resist the truth, and to rely upon the loquacity of human wisdom.'

*Encyclical "Quanta Cura,"*
*December 8, 1864*

### Abraham Lincoln

All this is not the result of accident. It has a philosophical cause. Without the *Constitution* and the Union, we could not have attained the result; but even these, are not the primary cause of our great prosperity. There is something back of these, entwining itself more closely about the human heart. That something is the principle of 'Liberty to all'—the principle that clears the *path* for all—gives *hope* to all—and, by consequence, *enterprise* and *industry* to all. . . . No oppressed people will *fight,* and *endure,* as our fathers did, without the promise of something better than a mere change of masters.

*The Constitution and the Union, 1860*

### Pope Pius IX

Meanwhile we shall not cease daily to direct our humble prayers to the Father of light and the God of all consolation, to the end that all obstacles being overcome, the counsels of

## Appendix

the enemies of religious and social order turned to nought, political passions calmed, her full liberty restored to the spouse of Jesus Christ, the Mexican nation may be enabled to hail in the person of your Majesty, its father, its regenerator, and its greatest and most imperishable glory.

*Letter to Emperor Maximilian,
October 18, 1864*

### ABRAHAM LINCOLN

The world will little note, nor long remember what we say here, but it can never forget what they did here. It is for us the living, rather, to be dedicated here to the unfinished work which they who fought here have thus far so nobly advanced. It is rather for us to be here dedicated to the great task remaining before us—that from these honored dead we take increased devotion to that cause for which they gave the last full measure of devotion—that we here highly resolve that these dead shall no have died in vain—that this nation, under God, shall have a new birth of freedom—and that government of the people, by the people, for the people, shall not perish from the earth.

*Gettysburg Address,
November 19, 1863*

### ABRAHAM LINCOLN

With malice toward none; with charity for all; with firmness in the right as God gives us to see the right; let us strive on to finish the work that we are in; to bind up the Nation's wounds; to care for him who shall have borne the battle, and for his widow and his orphan—to do all which may achieve and cherish a just and lasting peace among ourselves and with all nations.

*Second Inaugural Address,
March 4, 1865*

# Notes

*Preface*

1. Charles Chiniquy: *Fifty Years in the Church of Rome*, Fleming H. Revell Co., New York, 1886.

*Chapter One: The Shot That Echoes Unceasingly*

1. Carl Sandburg: *Abraham Lincoln, The Prairie Years*, Harcourt Brace, New York, 1929, p. 341.
2. Will Durant: *The Age of Faith*, Simon and Schuster, New York, 1950, p. 784.

*Chapter Two: The Theory That Justified the Act*

1. *Pontificale Romanum Summorum Pontificum*, Pope Benedict XV edition, H. Dessain, Mechlin, Belgium, 1934.
2. St. Thomas Aquinas, *Summa Theologica*, Louis Guerin, Barri-Ducis, 1857, Tomus Quartus, Quaestio XI, Articulus III, p. 90.
3. *Idem.*
4. *Catholic Encyclopedia*, Encyclopedia Press, London, 1911, Vol. XII, p. 443, "Probabilism."
   Henry Davis, S. J.: *Moral Theology*, Sheed & Ward, New York, 1952, p. 8.
   H. Noldin, S. J.: *Summa Theologiae Moralis*, Frederick Pustet Co., New York, 1952, pp. 235 ff.
   H. Jone: *Moral Theology*, Newman Press, Westminister, Md., 1952, p. 45.
5. *Catholic Encyclopedia, op. cit.*, Vol. XII, p. 442.

6. Edwin Sherman: *Engineer Corps of Hell,* privately printed, 1883, p. 47.
7. Hoensbroech, Count von: *Fourteen Years a Jesuit,* Cassell & Co., London, 1911, Vol. II, p. 328.

*Chapter Three: Backdrop for Treason*

1. *Arizona Register,* June 30, 1961.
2. *Ibid.,* September 30, 1960.
3. Justin H. Smith: *The War with Mexico,* Macmillan Co., New York, 1919, Vol. I, pp. 391, 393, 395, 494, 527, 550; Vol. II, p. 81.
4. *Ibid.,* Vol. I, p. 494.
5. *Ibid.,* Vol. II, p. 81.
6. *Ibid.*
7. John T. Christian: *America or Rome, Which?,* Baptist Book Concern, Louisville, Ky., 1895, p. 86.
8. John J. Meng and E. J. Gergely: *American History for Catholic High Schools,* W. A. Sadlier, Inc., New York, 1954, p. 230.
9. Samuel B. Morse: *Foreign Conspiracy Against the Liberties of the United States,* Leavitt, Lord & Co., New York, 1835, pp. 84-5.
10. *Ibid.,* p. 86.
11. *Appleton's American Annual Cyclopaedia,* New York, Vol. V, 1865, p. 749.
12. Leonard Patrick O'Connor Wibberley: *The Coming of the Green,* Henry Holt and Co., New York, 1958, p. 53.
13. *Idem.*
14. *Ibid.,* p. 54.
15. *Ibid.,* p. 85.
16. *Ibid.,* p. 88.
17. *Ibid.,* p. 95.
18. *Arizona Register,* April 21, 1961.
18a. Lenoir Chambers: *Stonewall Jackson,* Wm. Morrow Co., New York, 1959, p. 426.
18b. *Ibid.,* p. 143.
19. J. T. Headly: *Great Riots of New York 1712-1873,* E. B. Treat, New York, 1873, pp. 149 ff.
Wibberley, *op. cit.,* pp. 81-6.
*New York Daily Tribune,* July 16, 17, and 18, 1863 (examined in New York Public Library).

## Notes

    *Harper's Weekly*, July 25, August 1, and August 8, 1863 (examined in the private collection of Mr. Samuel Fengel, Los Angeles).
    *Arizona Republic*, October 23, 1960.
    *Arizona Register*, September 30, 1960.
20. *Harper's Weekly*, August 1, 1863.
21. Headly, *op. cit.*, p. 207.
22. *New York Daily Tribune*, July 18, 1863.
23. *Idem.*
24. *Idem.*
25. *Harper's Weekly*, August 1, 1863.
26. *Arizona Register*, September 30, 1960.
    *Our Sunday Visitor*, September 24, 1961.
27. Headly, *op. cit.*, p. 187.
28. *New York Daily Tribune*, July 16, 1863.
29. *Ibid.*, July 18, 1863.
30. *Harper's Weekly*, August 1, 1863.

*Chapter Four: Conspiracy South of the Border*

1. A. R. Tyrner-Tyrnauer: *Lincoln and the Emperors*, Harcourt, Brace & World, New York, 1962, p. 73.
2. *Ibid.*, p. 123.
3. *Appleton's American Annual Cyclopaedia*, New York, Vol. III, 1863, p. 633.
4. *Idem.*
5. *Ibid.*, Vol. III, p. 644.
6. Ralph Roeder: *Juarez y su Mexico*, published by the author, Mexico City, 1958, Vol. I, pp. 491, 510, 511; Vol. II, p. 452.
7. Daniel Dawson: *The Mexican Adventure*, G. Bell & Sons, London, 1935, p. 58.
8. *Appleton's American Annual Cyclopaedia, op. cit.*, Vol. III, p. 641.
9. Dawson, *op. cit.*, p. 80.
10. *Ibid.*, p. 151.
11. *Ibid.*, p. 152.
12. *Ibid.*, p. 208.
13. *Idem.*
14. *Ibid.*, p. 209.
15. *Ibid.*, p. 210.
16. *Ibid.*, p. 211.

17. *Appleton's American Annual Cyclopaedia, op. cit.*, Vol. IV, pp. 526-7.
18. *Ibid.*, Vol. II, 1862, p. 746.
19. Tyrner-Tyrnauer, *op. cit.*, p. 21.
20. Dawson, *op. cit.*, p. 212.
21. *Idem*.
22. Leo Francis Stock: *United States Ministers to the Papal States*, Catholic University Press, Washington, D.C., 1933.
23. *Ibid.*, p. 324.
24. *Ibid.*, p. 344.
25. R. W. Thompson: *Footprints of the Jesuits*, Thomas Crowell Co., New York, 1894, pp. 229-31.
26. Tyrner-Tyrnauer, *op. cit.*, p. 62.
27. *Ibid.*, p. 63.
28. *Ibid.*, pp. 91, 92, 99.

*Chapter Five: The Man and the Demi-God*

1. Frederico Hoyos, S.V.D.: *Enciclicas Pontificias*, Editorial Guadalupe, Buenos Aires, 1958, p. 153.
2. *Appleton's American Annual Cyclopaedia, op. cit.*, Vol. III, p. 821.
3. Count Charles Arribavene: *Italy under Victor Emmanuel*, Hurst & Blackett, London, 1862, Vol. II, pp. 299-300.
4. John McKnight: *The Papacy: A New Appraisal*, Rinehart, New York, 1952, p. 205.
5. R. W. Thompson: *The Footprints of the Jesuits*, Thomas Y. Crowell & Co., New York, 1894, p. 306.
6. McKnight, *op. cit.*, p. 481.
7. *Ibid.*, p. 481.
8. G. S. Godkin: *Life of Victor Emmanuel II*, Macmillan & Co., London, 1880.
9. Arribavene, *op. cit.*, Vol. II, p. 389.
10. Denis Mack Smith: *Garibaldi*, Alfred Knopf, New York, 1956, p. 175.
11. Guillermo Dellhora: *La Iglesia Catolica ante la critica en el pensamiento y en el arte*, Ediciones Dellhora, Mexico City, 1929, p. 248.
12. Arribavene, *op. cit.*, Vol. II, p. 366.
13. Godkin, *op. cit.*, pp. 76-7.
14. Hoyos, *op. cit.*, p. 179.
15. John T. Christian: *America or Rome, Which?*, Baptist Book Concern, Louisville, Kent., 1895, pp. 130-1.

## Notes

*Chapter Seven: The Hired Hands A Motley Crew*

1. Burke McCarty: *The Suppressed Truth about the Assassination of Abraham Lincoln,* published by the author, Philadelphia, 1924, p. 98.
2. Theodore Roscoe: *The Web of Conspiracy,* Prentice-Hall, Englewood, N. J., 1960, p. 64.
3. *The Great Conspiracy,* Barclay & Co., Philadelphia, 1866, p. 161.
4. Joseph McCabe: *A History of the Popes,* Watts and Co., London, 1939, p. 481.
5. Stock, *op. cit.,* p. 343.
6. *The Great Conspiracy, op. cit.,* p. 168.
7. Roscoe, *op. cit.,* p. 48.
8. *Ibid.,* p. 45.
9. *Ibid.,* p. 47.
10. *Ibid.,* p. 121.
11. *Ibid.,* p. 243.
12. *Trial of John H. Surratt,* Government Printing Office, Washington, D.C., 1867, pp. 332-3.
13. Roscoe, *op. cit.,* p. 477.
14. T. M. Harris: *The Assassination of Lincoln: A History of the Great Conspiracy,* American Citizen Co., Boston, 1892, p. 208.
15. *Ibid.,* p. 100.
16. *Ibid.,* p. 103.
17. *Idem.*
18. *Ibid.,* p. 104.
19. McCarty, *op. cit.,* p. 110.
20. Harris, *op. cit.,* p. 105.
21. *Ibid.,* p. 104.
22. Roscoe, *op. cit.,* p. 58.
23. Harris, *op. cit.,* p. 104.
24. *Idem.*
25. Stock, *op. cit.,* p. 371.
26. Harris, *op. cit.*

*Chapter Eight: The Ancient Privilege of Sanctuary*

1. *Trial of John H. Surratt, op. cit.,* pp. 1351-2.
2. *Ibid.,* p. 898.

# Notes

3. United States Government, Executive Documents, 2d Session 39th Congress, Government Printing Office, Washington, D.C., 1866-7, p. 5.
4. Harris, *op. cit.*, pp. 218-9.
5. *Ibid.*, pp. 221-2.
6. See footnote 3, *supra*, p. 4.
7. Harris, *op. cit.*, p. 224.
8. Otto Eisenschiml: *In the Shadow of Lincoln's Death*, Wilfred Funk Co., New York, 1940, p. 236.
9. See footnote 3, *supra*, pp. 14-5.
10. Stock, *op. cit.*, p. 386.
11. Roscoe, *op. cit.*, p. 508.
12. *Ibid.*, p. 509.

*Chapter Nine: The Trial of John Surratt*

1. *Trial of John H. Surratt, op. cit.*, p. 1131.
2. McCarty, *op. cit.*, p. 190, and Harris, *op. cit.*, p. 249.
3. See footnote 1, *supra*, p. 990.
4. Eisenschiml, *op. cit.*, p. 275.
5. Harris, *op. cit.*, pp. 243-4.
6. *Ibid.*, p. 281.
7. See footnote 1, *supra*, pp. 851-2.
8. Harris, *op. cit.*, p. 281.
9. See footnote 1, *supra*, p. 149.
10. Harris, *op. cit.*, pp. 280-1.
11. See footnote 1, *supra*, p. 1211.
12. Alfred Isaacson, "John Surratt and the Lincoln Assassination Plot," *Maryland Historical Magazine*, Vol. 57, 1957, p. 341.

# *Bibliography*

The letters C, P, or N, in parentheses after a book, indicate that the viewpoint expressed by the author or publisher is primarily Catholic, Protestant, or Neutral.

*Abraham Lincoln: His Speeches and Writings,* by Roy P. Basler, World Publishing Co., Cleveland and New York, 1946 (N).
*Abraham Lincoln, the Prairie Years,* by Carl Sandburg, Harcourt, Brace & Co., New York, 1926 (N).
*Abraham Lincoln, the War Years,* by Carl Sandburg, Harcourt, Brace & Co., New York, 1942 (N).
*Adams-Jefferson Letters,* by Lester J. Cappon, University of North Carolina Press, Chapel Hill, N.C., 1959 (N).
*America or Rome, Which?,* by John T. Christian, Baptist Book Concern, Louisville, Ky., 1895 (P).
*American History for Catholic High Schools* by John Meng and E. J. Gergely, W. H. Sadlier Co., New York, 1955 (C).
*Appleton's American Annual Cyclopaedia,* New York, Vols. I-IV, 1861-4 (N).
*Argument of Hon. Edwards Pierrepont to the Jury, on the Trial of John H. Surratt for the Murder of President Lincoln,* Government Printing Office, Washington, D.C., 1867 (N).
*Arizona Register* (C).
*Arizona Republic* (N).

## Bibliography

*Assassination and History of the Conspiracy,* J. R. Hawley & Co., New York, 1865 (N).

*Assassination of Abraham Lincoln,* by Osborn H. Oldroyd, Washington, published by the author, 1901 (N).

*Assassination of Lincoln: A History of the Great Conspiracy,* by T. M. Harris, American Citizen Co., Boston, 1892 (P).

*Assassination of President Lincoln and the Trial of the Conspirators,* by Benn Pitman (court reporter), Funk and Wagnalls, New York, 1954 (N).

*Career and Adventures of John H. Surratt since His Flight from America, His Final Arrest in Egypt by U.S. Consul Hale,* by C. W. Alexander, Philadelphia, 1866 (N).

*Case for Mrs. Surratt,* by Helen Jones Campbell, G. P. Putnam's Sons, New York, 1943 (C).

*Case of Mary Surratt: Her Controversial Trial and Execution for Conspiracy in the Lincoln Assassination,* by Guy W. Moore, University of Oklahoma Press, Norman, Okla., 1954 (N).

*Catholic Church in the United States,* by Theodore Roemer, O.F.M. Cap., B. Herder Co., St. Louis, 1950 (C).

*Catholic Encyclopedia, Encyclopedia Press,* London, 1914 (C).

*Catholicity in Philadelphia,* by Joseph L. J. Kirlin, J. J. McVey, Philadelphia, 1909 (C).

*Church, State, and Freedom,* by Leo Pfeffer, Beacon Press, Boston, 1953 (N).

*Coming of the Green,* by Leonard Patrick O'Connor Wibberley, Henry Holt and Co., New York, 1958 (C).

*Day Lincoln Was Shot, The,* by Jim Bishop, Harper & Brothers, New York, 1955 (N).

*Death of Lincoln,* by Clara E. Laughlin, Doubleday Page & Co., 1909 (N).

*Death to Traitors,* by Jacob Mogelever, Doubleday & Co., New York, 1960 (N).

*Decay of the Church of Rome,* by Joseph McCabe, Methuen & Co., London, 1909 (P).

*Emergence of Liberal Catholicism in America, The,* by Robert D. Gross, Harvard University Press, Cambridge, Mass., 1958 (C).

## Bibliography

*Enchiridion Symbolorum*, by Henry Denziger, Herder, Barcelona, 1946 (C).
*Enciclicas Pontificas*, by Federico Hoyos, S.V.D., Editorial Guadalupe, Buenos Aires, Argentina, 1958 (C).
*Enciclopedia de la Religion Catolica*, by Dalmau y Jover, Barcelona, Spain, 1953 (C).
*Encyclopedia Britannica*, 13th ed., Britannica Co., Ltd., London, 1926 (N).
*Encyclopedia of the Papacy*, by Hans Kuehner, Philosophical Library, New York, 1958 (C).
*Engineer Corps of Hell*, by Edwin Sherman, privately printed, 1833 (P).
"Final Two Chapters in the Surratt Controversy," by Alfred Isaacson and Otto Eisenschiml, *Journal, Illinois State Historical Society*, Vol. 52, Summer 1959, pp. 279-90 (C and N).
*Fifty Years in the Church of Rome*, by Charles Chiniquy, Fleming H. Revell Co., New York, 1886 (P).
*Footprints of the Jesuits*, by R. W. Thompson, Hunt & Eaton, New York, 1894 (P).
*Foreign Conspiracy Against the Liberties of the United States*, by Samuel B. Morse, Leavitt, Lord & Co., New York, 1835 (P).
*Fourteen Years a Jesuit*, by Count Paul von Hoensbroech, Cassell & Co., Ltd., London, 1911 (P).
*Garibaldi*, by Denis Mack Smith, Alfred Knopf, New York, 1956 (N).
"General Rufus King and the Capture of John H. Surratt," by Duane Koenig, *Wisconsin Magazine of History*, Vol. 25, 1941, pp. 43-50 (N).
*Gracian's Manual*, by Baltasar Gracian, Charles C. Thomas, Springfield, Ill., 1934 (C).
*Great Conspiracy, The*, Barclay & Co., Philadelphia, 1866 (N).
*Great Conspiracy, The: Its Origin and History*, by John A. Logan, A. R. Hart & Co., New York, 1886 (N).
*Great Riots of New York 1712-1873*, by Hon. J. T. Headly, E. B. Treat, New York, 1873 (P).
*Harper's Weekly*, 1860-5 (N).

## Bibliography

*History of the Catholic Church in the United States,* by John Gilmary Shea, 4 vols., published by the author, New York, 1886-92 (C).

*History of the Papacy in the XIX Century,* by Dr. Fredric Nielsen, 2 vols., John Murray Co., London, 1906 (P).

*History of the Popes,* by Joseph McCabe, Watts & Co., London, 1939 (P).

*History of the United States Secret Service,* by Gen. Lafayette C. Baker, L. C. Baker, Pubr., Philadelphia, 1867 (N).

"*Humanus Genus*" *Against Freemasonry and the Spirit of the Age —and Reply,* Supreme Council, Scottish Rite, Washington, 1962 (P).

*Iglesia Catolica, La,* by Guillermo Dellhora, Ediciones Dellhora, Mexico City, 1929 (P).

*In the Shadow of Lincoln's Death,* by Otto Eisenschiml, Wilfred Funk Co., New York, 1940 (N).

*Italy under Victor Emmanuel,* by Count Charles Arribavene, Hurst & Blackett, London, 1862 (N).

*Jefferson Davis and His Complicity in the Assassination of Abraham Lincoln and Where the Traitor Shall Be Tried,* Sherman and Co., Philadelphia, 1866 (N).

*Jesuits, The,* by Theodor Griesinger, 2 vols., W. H. Allen & Co., London, 1883 (P).

"John Surratt and the Lincoln Assassination Plot," by Alfred Isaacson, *Maryland Historical Magazine,* Vol. 52, Dec. 1957, pp. 316-42 (C).

*Juarez y su Mejico,* by Ralph Roeder, Mexico City, 1958 (N).

*Judicial Murder of Mary E. Surratt,* by David Miller De Witt, J. Murphy & Co., Baltimore, 1895 (C).

*Life, Crime and Capture of John Wilkes Booth,* by George Alfred Townsend, Dick & Fitzgerald, New York, 1865 (N).

*Life of Abraham Lincoln,* by Ward H. Lamon, Osgood & Co., Boston, 1872 (N).

*Life of Victor Emmanuel II,* by G. S. Godkin, Macmillan & Co., London, 1880 (N).

## Bibliography

*Lincoln and the Emperors*, by A. R. Tyrner-Tyrnauer, Harcourt, Brace & World, Inc., New York, 1962 (N).

*Lo que es y lo que no es la Masoneria*, by Dr. Francisco Vela Gonzalez, Monterey, Mexico, 1960 (P).

*Mad Booths of Maryland, The*, by Stanley Kimmel, Bobbs-Merrill Co., New York, 1940 (N).

*Man Who Killed Lincoln, The*, by Philip Van Doren Stern, Dell Publishing Co. New York, 1955 (N).

*Maximilian and Carlotta*, by Count Egon Caesar Corti, New York, 1928 (N).

*Mejico a traves de los Siglos*, by Vicente Riva Palacia, Mexico City, 1887 (N).

*Mexican Adventure, The*, by Daniel Dawson, G. Bell & Sons, London, 1935 (N).

*Moral Theology*, by Herbert Jone, Newman Press, Westminster, Md., 1952 (C).

*New York Tribune*, 1860-5 (N).

*Our Sunday Visitor* (C).

*Papacy, The—A New Appraisal*, by John P. McKnight, Rinehart & Co., New York, 1952 (N).

*Papacy in the XIX Century, The*, by Friedrich Nippold, G. P. Putnam Sons, New York & London, 1900 (P).

*Papal Encyclicals*, by Anna Freemantle, New American Library, 1956 (C).

*Phantom Crown*, by Bertita Harding, Ediciones Toltuca, Mexico, 1960 (N).

*Popular History of the Catholic Church*, by Phillip Hughes, Doubleday & Co., New York, 1960 (C).

*Power and Secret of the Jesuits*, by René Fülop-Miller, George Braziller, New York, 1956 (C).

*Prince Napoleon in America, 1861*, by Georges Joyanx, Indiana University Press, Bloomington, Inc., 1959 (N).

*Roman Catholicism*, by Loraine Boettner, Presbyterian & Reform Pub. Co., Philadelphia, 1962 (P).

*Rome and the Newest Fashions in Religion*, by Hon. W. E. Gladstone, M. P., Harpers, New York, 1875 (P).

# Bibliography

*Slavery and Catholicism,* by Richard R. Miller, North State Pub. Co., Durham, N.C., 1957 (P).

*Spies, Traitors and Conspirators of the Late Civil War,* by Gen. Lafayette C. Baker, John E. Porter & Co., Philadelphia, 1894 (N).

*Stanton,* by Benjamin P. Thomas and Harold Hyman, Alfred Knopf, New York, 1962 (N).

*Stonewall Jackson,* by Lenoir Chambers, Wm. Morrow Co., New York, 1959 (N).

*Story of American Catholicism, The,* by Theodore Maynard, Macmillan and Co., New York, 1941 (C).

*Story of Mary Surratt,* play in three acts, by John Patrick (Goggan), Dramatists Play Service, New York, 1947 (C).

*Summa Theologia Moralis,* by H. Noldin, Frederick Pustet Co., New York, 1952 (C).

*Summa Theologica,* by St. Thomas Aquinas, L. Guerin Pub., Bar-Le-Duc, France, 1867 (C).

*Suppressed Truth about the Assassination of Abraham Lincoln, The,* by Burke McCarty, published by the author, Philadelphia, 1924 (P).

*This Is What We Found,* by Ralph and Carl Creger, Lyle Stuart, New York, 1960 (N).

*To the Golden Door,* by George Potter, Little Brown & Co., Boston, 1960 (C).

*Traicion de Queretaro,* by Alfonso Junco, Editorial Campeador, Mexico, 1956 (N).

*Trial of the Alleged Assassins and Conspirators at Washington, D.C., May and June, 1865, for the Murder of President Abraham Lincoln* . . . being a full and verbatim report, T. B. Peterson & Bros., Philadelphia, 1865 (N).

*Trial of the Conspirators for the Assassination of President Lincoln.* Argument of J. A. Bingham, Delivered June 27 and 28, 1865, before the Military Commission, Government Printing Office, Washington, D.C., 1865 (N).

*Trial of John H. Surratt in the Criminal Court for the District of*

## Bibliography

*Columbia,* Hon. G. P. Fisher presiding, 2 vols., Government Printing Office, Washington, D.C., 1867 (N).

*Trial of John H. Surratt . . . on an Indictment for Murder of President Lincoln,* R. Sutton, Washington, D.C., 1867 (N).

*Under Orders,* by William Sullivan, Richard Smith, New York, 19– (P).

*Union of Italy,* by Cecil Scott Forester, Dodd, New York, 1927 (N).

*United States Government, Executive Documents of the House of Representatives, Second Session of the Thirty-ninth Congress, 1866-7,* Government Printing Office, 1867, Serial Volume 1288 (N).

*United States Government. Department of State. Message from the President, Transmitting a Report . . . Relating to the Discovery and Arrest of John H. Surratt.* Washington, D.C., 1866 (N).

*United States Ministers to the Papal States,* by Leo Francis Stock, Catholic University Press, Washington, 1933 (C).

*War with Mexico, The,* by Justin H. Smith, Macmillan & Co., New York, 1919, Vols. I and II (N).

*Web of Conspiracy, The,* by Theodore Roscoe, Prentice-Hall, Englewood, N.J., 1960 (N).

*Why Was Lincoln Murdered?,* by Otto Eisenschiml, Little Brown, Boston, 1937 (N).

# Index

Agostina, J., pseudonym of J. Surratt, 144
Alhama, 93
Almonte, Gen., 73
Angola, Jesuits in, 84
Antonelli, Cardinal, 64, 75, 79, 143, 144, 146, 155
Aquinas, St. Thomas, 31
Argentina, 84, 87
Arizona, Jesuits in, 84
Arnold, S., 123-4, 127
Arribavene, Count C., 93-6
Assassination, Church attitude toward, 26-27
Atzerodt, G., 105, 111, 115-6, 122-4, 126, 158
Austria, Jesuits in, 84

Bach, Baron, 75
Bailey, A., 7
Baird, Rear Adm. G. W., 112
Baltimore plot, 103
Banks, J. P., 50
Barnes, Surgeon Gen., 112
Beauregard, Fr., 46, 131
Becan, Fr. M., 35
Belgium, in New World, 77-78
Belgrado, M., 87
Bellarmine, St. Robert, 35
Benedict XIV, 84
Bismarck, O. von, 90
Bolivar, Simon, 25, 87

Bolivia, 21, 87
Bonaparte, Capt., 77
Booth, John Wilkes, 16, 18, 36, 103-4, 107, 110, 111-6, 119-21, 123-4, 126, 136, 142, 145, 149, 158, 159
Boucher, Fr., 130-3, 135
Boyle, Fr. F. E., 119
Bradley, J. H., 147
Bradley, J. H., Jr., 147
Brazil, Church in, 77, 84
British royalty, plot against, 84
Budenz, L., 9
Burnette, Alexis, 149

Calvin, J., 22
Canada, "invasion" of, 48-9
  Roman Catholics in, 77
Carrington, E. C., 152
Catholic Church
  Lincoln's death and, 17-9
  and slavery, 21
  opposition to democracy, 23-4
  in Latin America, 25-6
  during Inquisition, 26-7
  on heresy, 29
  on assassination, 30ff.
  theories of, 31-7
  on loyalty to U.S.A., 38ff.
  in Mexican War, 39-42
  denounced by Morse, 42-5

# Index

Catholic Church
  in Draft riots, 46*ff*.
  in Mexico, 64-88
  and the Confederacy, 78-9
  in Colombia, 92-3
  connections with assassins, 110*ff*.
  and Booth, 111-5
  and M. Surratt, 116-9
  and J. Surratt, 119-20
  and Herold, 121-2
  and Dr. Mudd, 122-3
  and Arnold, 123-4
  and O'Laughlin, 124
  and Wiechman, 125-6
  protects Surratt, 129-44
  at Surratt trial, 145-55
  at Surratt funeral, 155-6
  involvement in assassination, 161-3
  Pius IX contrasted with Lincoln, 165-72
Cavour, C., 66
Chaillu, Dr., 86
Chile, 84, 87
Chiniquy, C., 8, 9, 19-20, 91, 162
Civil War Draft riots, *see* Draft riots
Clement XIV, 84
Coburgs, 73
Colombia, 84, 87, 92-4, 155
Comitolo, Fr. P., 35
Compensationism, 33
Confederacy, attitude of Church toward, 42, 78-9
Cortez, 21
Corwin, T., 71
Crowninshield, W. W., 112
Cuba, 84, 87

Dashills, J. H., 124
Davis, Jefferson, 16, 65, 78, 79, 109, 120, 142, 153, 159
De Molay, 22

Desertions from Army, 47-8
Draft Law, 51
Draft riots, 7, 46*ff*.
Dunn, Rev. J. E., 157
Durant, Will, 26-7
Dye, Sgt. J. M., 130, 152

Ecuador, 21, 84, 87
Elizabeth of England, 22
Emancipation Proclamation, 20, 51, 71
Emerson, R. W., 46
Encyclopedists, 22
Equiprobabilism, 33
Estrada, M. G. de, 71
Eugenie, Empress, 86

Fernandino, C, 103
Fisher, G. P., 150-1, 156
Fitzpatrick, Honora, 118
Fourth vow of Jesuits, 29
France, in New World, 78
  Jesuits in, 84
Francis, D., 9
Franco, on Freemasonry, 87
Franco-Prussian War, 90
Franz Joseph, 9, 36, 65-7, 73, 87, 90, 162, 164
Freemasonry, 10, 22-4, 86

Garibaldi, G., 25, 66, 93
Garnett, Fr., 84
Garrett, R., 16, 104
Garrity, M., 47-8
Georgetown College, 37, 50, 85
Gerard, Fr., 84
Gettysburg, battle of, 20, 55-6
Gingnare, Fr. J., 35
Goa, Jesuits in, 84
Gonzalez, T., 34
Grant, U. S., 104-5, 124, 159
Greeley, Horace, 59

187

# Index

Greenway, Fr., 84
Gregory XIV, 171
Guatemala, Jesuits in, 84
Gunpowder plot, 84

Hale, Charles, 144
Hapsburgs, 66, 73
Hardy, E. T., 87
*Harper's Weekly*, 15, 55, 62
Harris, T. M., 127-8, 139, 152
Henry VIII, 22
Herold, D., 104, 115-6, 121-3, 127, 158
Hevey, Fr., 131
Hidalgo, Jose, 24, 73
Hitler, on Freemasonry, 87
Holohan, J., 118
Holt, Judge Advocate General J., 120
Hughes, Archbishop John, 57-62, 83, 113, 161
Hull, *see* Paine, L.
Hus, John, 27
Hyman, H. M., 160

Immigrants, 44. *See also* Irish-Americans
Inca civilization, 21
Index of Forbidden Books, 22
Innocent III, 23
Innocent XI, 84
Innocent XIII, 84
Inquisition, 27-8, 110
Irisarri, Archbishop, 50
Irish-Americans, 38*ff*.
Irish Draft riots, *see* Draft riots
Italy, Jesuits in, 83, 84
Italy, unification of, 37, 90, 94, 155

Jackson, Stonewall, 50

Jesuits
in history, 27-8
theories of, 29-37
in Civil War, 50
in Mexico, 67*ff*., 84
banned in Europe, 84-5
on Freemasonry, 86-8
and Italian unity, 90, 93-9
contrasted with Lincoln, 89*ff*.
in behalf of Surratt, 146*ff*.
Joan of Arc, 27, 110
John VIII, 26
John, King of England, 23
Johnson, A., 16, 18, 30, 103, 105, 109, 117, 122, 156, 158-60
Juarez, B., 25, 67*ff*., 80, 87, 90, 110. *See also* Maximilian

King, Rufus, 79, 83, 107, 114, 125, 140-4

Lincoln, A.
mourning for, 13-5
Church opposition to, 19-21
contrasted with Pius IX, 89*ff*., 165-72
assassination described, 103-5
assassins described, 107-28
Lincoln, Mary, 16
Loosey, Carl F. von, 64-5
Luther, M., 22
Lynch, Bishop, 42, 113-4

Magna Carta, 23
Mariana, Fr. J., 34-6
Marti, J., 87
Masonic Orders, *see* Freemasonry
Mastai-Ferretti, G., *see* Pius IX
Matamoras, 93
Maximilian, Emperor, 9, 67*ff*., 73*ff*., 90, 92, 153, 164, 172

# Index

Mazzini, G., 25, 66, 96
McCarthy, pseud. of Surratt, 135
McClermont, Mrs. 145
McElroy, Rev. J., 44
McNamara, Eugene, 40-2
Medina, Bartholomew, 34
Meese, N., 10
Melville, H., 15
Menu, Fr. John, 151
Merrick, R. I., 147, 152-5
Metternich, R., 66, 73
Mexico, Indians in, 21
    struggles of, 24-5
    war with U.S.A., 40-2, 50
    conspiracy in, 64-88
    Jesuits in, 84
    *See also* Juarez, Maximilian
Miller, H., 10
Missouri, Constitution of, 45
Monarchy plans for U.S., 64
Monroe Doctrine, 9
Montezuma, 21
Morales, 25
Moreno, M., 87
Mormons, 88
Morse, S. B., 42-4, 45
Mudd, Dr. S., 104, 112, 117, 121-3, 127, 158-9
Murder, Church attitude toward, 30*ff*.

Nagle, S. B., 149, 151
Naples, Jesuits in, 84
Napoleon III, 1-2, 9, 36, 57, 65-7, 73-4, 77, 86, 90, 153, 164
Nast, T., 15
Neane, Fr., 139
New Granada, *see* Colombia
New Mexico, Jesuits in, 84

O'Brien, D., 47
O'Higgins, B., 87
O'Laughin, M., 123, 124, 127, 158

Oliva, Gen., 34
O'Mahoney, John, 48
O'Neill, John, 48, 49
O'Regan, Bishop, 8, 20

Paine, L., 104, 115-6, 118-21, 123-4, 126-7, 158
Paraguay, 87
Parma, Jesuits in, 84
Patricians, *see* San Patricios
Payne, L., *see* Paine, L.
Pedro II, 73
Peru, 21, 28, 84, 87
Peru, Catholic Church in, 28
Philippines, Jesuits in, 84
Pierrepont, E., 130-3, 145, 152
Pius IX, 9, 23, 36-7, 57, 64-88, 89*ff*., 143-4, 146, 153-5, 162, 164, 166-72. *See also* Catholic Church
Porterfield, accomplice of Surratt, 130
Portugal, Jesuits in, 84
Potter, J. F., 134-5
Powell, *see* Paine, L.
Probabiliorism, 33
Probabilism, 32
Protestantism in U.S.A., 22
Puerto Rico, Jesuits in, 84

Rathbone, Major, 104
Reconstruction movement, 16
Regicide, Jesuits on, 34*ff*.
Riots, *see* Draft riots
Roman Catholic Church, *see* Catholic Church
Romero, Matias, 71

Sa, Fr. E., 35
Ste. Marie, H. B., 107, 125, 139-43, 151
Salazar, on Freemasonry, 87

189

# Index

Sanctuary of Surratt, 129*ff*.
Sandburg, C., 20
San Marin, 87
San Patricios, 39
Santa Anna, Gen., 40-1
Savonarola, 27, 110
Scribanus, Fr. C., 35
Seward, W. H., 16, 78-9, 83, 104, 114, 121, 134-6, 143, 159
Seymour Gov., 58
Sicily, Jesuits in, 84
Slavery, Church attitude toward, 20-2
   Irish attitude toward, 45*ff*.
Smith, Capt. H. W., 118
Smith, John, 22
Society of Jesus, *see* Jesuits
Spain, Jesuits in, 84
Spangler, E., 104, 124-7, 158
Stanton, E. M., 16, 18, 109, 158-60
Stonestreet, Fr. C. H., 119
Suarez, Fr. F., 35
Sucre, 87
Surratt, Anna, 30, 118, 119, 155
Surratt, Isaac, 117
Surratt, J., 19, 37, 85, 107, 116, 118, 123, 125, 126, 158-60, 162-3
   part in conspiracy, 119-20
   escape aided by Church, 129*ff*.
   in Vatican, 139-44
   apprehension of, 140-4
   trial of, 145-55
   amnesty of, 155
   becomes Catholic teacher, 155
   funeral of, 155-6
Surratt, John, Sr., 118
Surratt, Mary, 30, 85, 103, 110, 115-20, 122-3, 126, 128, 141-2, 154, 155, 158-9, 160, 164

Sweeney, "Fighting Tom," 48

Tanner, Fr. A., 35
Thomas, B. P., 160
Thomas, St., *see* Aquinas
Thoreau, H., 46
Trent, Council of, 98
Trigo, 93
Turner-Tyrnauer, A. R., 64
Tutiorism, 33

Uruguay, 87

Valera, Eamon de, 48
Vatican, *see* Catholic Church
Venezuela, 87
Victor Emmanuel, 25, 66, 83, 90, 97-9, 146

Walter, Fr. J. A., 119, 128
Ward, Anna, 126
Watson, John pseud. of Surratt, 139-40, 141
Washington, George, 23
Welsh, Judge, 53
Wesley, J., 22
Whitman, W., 13
Wibberley, L. P. O., 46, 47
Wiechman, L. J., 107, 117-8, 122, 125, 141-2
Wilding, H., 135, 137
Wood, L., *see* Paine, L.

Young, Fr. W. D., 119

Zwingli, U., 22